The Shadow in the Wind

Lazaros
Zigomanis

First published by Pinion Press 2019

ISBN
Print: 978-0-6484789-0-4
Ebook: 978-1-925830-83-5

This is a work of fiction. Any similarities between places and characters are a coincidence.

Cover image: Kev Howlett, Busybird Publishing
Cover design: Blaise van Hecke, Busybird Publishing
Layout and typesetting: Busybird Publishing

Pinion Press
2/118 Para Road
Montmorency, Victoria
Australia 3094

Pinion Press is an imprint of Busybird Publishing

www.busybird.com.au

To never giving up hope.

Dad

Keene sat at the upright piano, left hand hovering over the coloured pencils scattered across the piano lid. He grabbed the yellow pencil and, tongue poking from the side of his mouth, coloured in the sun.

'What do you think, Bunch?' he asked.

He swivelled on the piano stool, feet dangling above the floor, and held his picture up to Bunch. Curled on the couch, the Border Collie pricked his ears, and tilted his head. His tail thumped the cushion.

Keene put his picture back on the piano lid. The sun blazing in the blue sky was perfect. As was the house with its neat rose garden, and the big gum tree in front. He frowned at the tyre swing – a dark, angry splotch of black. He ran his fingers over it, felt the dent in the paper. It would have to do. Still, something was missing.

The stairs in the hall creaked. 'Keene?'

'Yes, Dad!'

'Just checking.'

Footsteps continued down the hall and receded into the kitchen. Then the radio came on, soft and crackly, spluttering out one of those hard rock songs with lots of guitars and drums that Dad liked so much. Then it hit Keene. Of course – Dad's van was missing from the picture! Keene reached for the red pencil, but stopped when he heard the screen door screech open. A knock on the front door followed.

Bunch was a blur of black and white as he leaped from the couch, paws skittering across the floor. Keene put his pencil down and hopped from the stool – knocking clear the roof tile that kept the practice pedal depressed – and chased after him.

'Bunch, quiet!' Keene said. 'Sshhh! Mum's sleeping! Down!'

Bunch lay down on his belly, his tail swishing back and forth.

Keene opened the door to find a man too big for the doorway, his shadow stretching down the hall. His face was stony, with a long, thick beard, and he wore a black suit and a white shirt that were creaseless, the only splash of colour a red tie.

'Hello there, young man,' he said, and dropped to one knee. His eyes were slate – a wall that hid his feelings. 'What's your name?'

'K–Keene.'

'I'm Mr. Obling.'

Mr. Obling's hand swallowed Keene's up in a handshake. Bunch leaped to his feet, muzzle twitching.

'And how old are you, Keene?'

Keene went blank.

'Answer him, Keene.'

Dad emerged from the kitchen and strode down the long, narrow hall, his boots clopping across the hardwood floor. His skin was leathery, darker than his sandy hair, and he was tall and hard and rigid. The left strap of his overalls flapped loose as he walked. It had been a long time since Mum had last sewn it.

'Six,' Keene said. '*Almost* seven!'

Dad's hands rested on Keene's shoulders. Keene drew himself up. Bunch's ears relaxed.

'Aren't you a big boy?' Mr. Obling said, pulling his hand clear and rubbing his palm as if Keene's handshake had been too tight.

Keene grinned.

'I'm very pleased to meet you,' Mr. Obling said. He rose up and offered a handshake above Keene's head. 'Mr. Hayes?'

Dad nodded. 'Nolan. Nolan Hayes.' He shook Mr. Obling's hand once. 'We spoke on the phone. Come in. Keene, move please.'

Keene stepped aside as Mr. Obling ambled into the house.

'This way,' Dad said.

He led Mr. Obling down the hall. Keene didn't want to get in their way, so he ran through the dining room and to the archway that also connected to the kitchen. Mr. Obling was just sitting down in a chair, his legs so long they couldn't fold under the kitchen table. Dad turned off the radio and filled the kettle.

'Kee,' he said, 'why don't you take Bunch outside? Mr. Obling and I have some things to discuss.'

Keene continued to gawp at Mr. Obling.

'Kee? Now, please.'

'Okay, Dad.'

Keene bolted across the kitchen and down the hall, skidding to a halt in front of the door. His shoes and slippers lay haphazardly on the floor, among Dad's good shoes and his boots, and several pairs of Mum's shoes – although she hadn't worn any of them for a while. They sat now abandoned, gathering dust, with a spider web stretched between the heel and sole of one. Keene grabbed his shoes, pulled them on, and pushed through the screen door.

The wind chimes hanging above the veranda jangled and the leaves on the gum tree that was the yard's centrepiece fluttered. Branches mushroomed against the window of Keene's bedroom, while those opposite intertwined with the gum's twin that stood misshapen amidst the eucalypti that rimmed the property. It made it impossible to tell from which tree the tyre swing – the knot that held it frayed, and always a point of contention between Mum and Dad – hung, while Dad's hammock swayed between the two.

Keene hugged himself. It wasn't late, but the sky bulged with darkening clouds, the last remnants of sunlight just tapering streamers. He should get a jacket. Mum would insist. Her voice rang in his head.

The roses that filled the flowerbed shook in a chorus of agreement. They were so unruly they engulfed the veranda's spindles. A pair of clippers were half-buried in the dirt, as well as a rusty trowel. Sometimes Keene would hold the clippers and Mum would guide his hand as they pruned the roses. When they were done, Mum would throw her arms around him, kiss his temple, and tell him he had a green thumb. Keene checked his hand once and told her she was wrong, and she laughed and hugged him tighter.

The roses needed more than pruning now. Their petals were splotched and the stems drooped, like the flowers themselves had doubled over in exhaustion. He wasn't sure where to start or whether he should, but it could be a nice surprise for Mum if he could get them right.

Something small and dark moved from behind the blade of the trowel – a spider, the peaks of its legs pointed, its body thick and bulbous. It lifted its foreleg, preparing to charge. Dad always killed spiders he found in the house, although Mum caught them and let them loose in the garden.

Keene grabbed the handle of the trowel. The soil under the spider trembled. The spider burst. Countless tiny spiders flooded from its back. Keene stumbled, fell on his behind, and scrambled to his feet. The tiny spiders swarmed the mother. He gagged, spun, and froze.

A dirt road, a mohawk of grass running down its centre, wound from the gum trees and all the way to the dilapidated garage tacked onto the house. Parked outside the garage was Dad's old red van; behind it was Averil's yellow bug, splattered with mud; behind that was Mr. Obling's car, a long black station wagon with gold floral script stencilled across the front door.

Keene had never seen a car with words on it. He ran up and tried to sound them out, but they were too big, and the flowing letters confused him. He fixed on the three letters that started the second word.

'*Fun*,' he said. The word continued, but the only other letters he could make out were the last two. '*Al*. Fun-al?'

Something cold nuzzled at his hand – Bunch. A tennis ball lay in the grass under the tyre swing, almost camouflaged among the fallen leaves. Keene grabbed the ball and threw it against the misshapen gum. Bunch hurled himself through the air to catch it, then brought it back. Again and again, Keene threw the ball, laughing, until he missed his target and the ball plunged behind the line of the trees.

Bunch raced to the perimeter of the yard, then stopped.

'Go get it, Bunch!'

Bunch did not move.

'Go, boy!'

Bunch lowered onto his front elbows and his tail wagged. Keene took a step forward. Bunch whirled on the spot. Keene drew closer. He could see the ball behind the misshapen gum's trunk. Dad's warnings – about wandering off and getting lost – rang in his mind. Keene was sure he wouldn't. During the summer, he, Mum, and Dad hiked to Miller's Pond for a picnic. Keene was sure he knew the bush well.

He glanced at his weatherboard house with its planks that needed painting and roof that needed tiles replaced. Light shone through the screen door from the kitchen. Above it, Mum's bedroom window was as dark as all the others. Keene's bedroom window was lost behind the branches of the gum tree. The wind chimes clanged louder.

Bunch barked.

'Get it, Bunch!'

Bunch span.

'Go, boy, get it!'

Bunch did not move.

Keene braced himself – it wouldn't be so bad just to get the ball. It wasn't very far at all.

He stepped out from the yard and into the trees. Everything became dark and muffled. He picked up his tennis ball and turned as lightning flashed. The knotted bark twisted into a face framed by clumps of hair. Keene fell back a step. But then it was gone, leaving nothing but the streams of bark.

Holding his breath, Keene reached forward until his fingertips were almost on the trunk. A tremendous boom filled his ears. He shrieked and snatched back his hand. But it was only thunder. Rain followed.

Bunch leaped into the trees and nipped around him, perhaps trying to herd him out.

'Kee! Kee, you get back here!'

It was Dad, now on the veranda with Mr. Obling. Keene sprinted towards them, Bunch by his side.

'I told you to stay in the yard!'

'I had to get the ball, Dad!'

Keene waved the ball as he hopped onto the veranda. Dad snatched the ball from him and threw it into the yard. Bunch span back and forth, unsure whether to chase the ball or to stay with Keene.

'I've told you never to leave the yard,' Dad said. 'You'll get lost. Now, inside! Get a towel from the bathroom and dry yourself.'

Keene nodded, fearing a swat on the bottom that never came.

'Bunch, too!'

Keene went back into the house – Bunch close behind him – and kicked off his shoes. Averil was already striding down the hall, a towel in one hand, a cup of tea in the other. She was a tall, dark woman, her black hair like lines of tightly-coiled springs. When Dad first hired her several months ago, Keene had found her so different that she intimidated him. But he'd since learned everything about her was calm:

from her pastel outfits, to her melodic voice, to the way she seemed to glide when she walked.

'My goodness,' she said, dropping the towel on Keene's head and tousling his hair. 'You should know better.'

'The ball got lost.'

'You finish drying. Your mother will want to see you soon.'

She released the towel and scooted upstairs, the stairs failing to sound a single creak. It made the house feel empty and quiet, but for the patter of rain, Bunch panting, and – outside – Dad talking to Mr. Obling.

'… just down the road, Mr. Hayes,' Mr. Obling was saying. 'It can't be more than five minutes away.'

'We already own plots there,' Dad said. 'My wife wanted to organise all this … to spare us …'

'It is probably the best place to take her.'

Keene cocked his head. Mr. Obling was going to take Mum? He wasn't Doctor Ward. What did he want with her?

'It's the most convenient site,' Mr. Obling went on. 'Although its closeness may be difficult.'

'I drive past every morning when I take Keene to school, and every afternoon when I pick him up,' Dad said. 'This is difficult regardless.'

'I understand, Mr. Hayes.'

Keene kneeled beside Bunch and rubbed the towel up and down Bunch's body as Dad and Mr. Obling exchanged farewells. The screen door swung open. Dad froze, holding the door ajar. A bitter breeze gusted through the hall like an unwelcome guest determined to intrude. Keene shivered.

'I thought I told you to go into the bathroom,' Dad said.

'Averil brought me a towel.'

Dad let out a long breath. He released the screen door. 'Kee, if I ask you to do something, please do it, okay?'

'Okay.'

'Nolan?' It was Averil at the top of the stairs. 'Deidre is ready to see Keene.'

'Thanks, Averil,' Dad said. 'Okay, go see your mum.'

Keene nodded and bolted up the stairs, Bunch close behind.

Pendant

The door to Mum's bedroom squealed as Keene opened it. Averil turned, startled, but Mum smiled – her delight was all Keene saw.

'We really need to get Nolan to fix that door,' Averil said.

'I barely notice it anymore,' Mum said.

She lay in bed, tubes coming out of her arm and leading up to a bag of clear liquid hanging from a metal pole with a little machine attached. Keene wasn't sure what it was. Dad said the stuff in the bag made Mum feel better, although if it did that, that didn't explain why she was always in bed.

Keene bounced on his heels, hands clasped behind his back, waiting obediently – he had to wait, to make sure Averil was finished. Bunch sauntered up behind him and lay before the doorway, front legs outstretched and tail swiping the floor.

'You know what to do,' Mum said.

In the corner a small, old stereo – its silver finish now faded to a dull grey – sat on a dresser, perched among a mound of scattered CDs. Keene switched the stereo on. The LCD screen revealed two dashes and the stereo emitted a steady low whine, like it was unhappy to be awakened.

'There's nothing in there,' Keene said.

'Hmmm,' Mum said. 'How about number twenty-one today?'

Keene rummaged through the CDs, struggling to read their titles, although he recognised the likenesses emblazoned across their covers, as well as the shape of words – *Mozart, Beethoven, Bach,* among others – that were as familiar as his own name. Then he found it: Mozart's Piano Concerto 21. He slid the CD into the player, and pushed PLAY. A familiar melody filled the room.

'That's it.' Mum patted the bedside.

Keene clambered up. The room was colder than the rest of the house. And dark. Dad said it was because of the way the gum tree outside shielded the window from the sun, but it *always* seemed dark –

especially the far corner, where shadows writhed. The only colour was on the wall by the door where all the pictures Keene had drawn for Mum had been stuck side by side.

Mum ran her hand up and down Keene's back. Keene kissed her on the cheek. She didn't smell the same anymore – not like she used to, like strawberries and the hot scones that would come out of the oven on Sunday mornings. There was something else now, although Keene couldn't identify it.

She was thin, too, her cheekbones sharp, her chin pointed, and even her sternum poked out where the nightgown exposed her bare chest. Her once golden hair was now dank and thin. She placed the hand with the tubes in it on her chest, her fingers opening and closing.

'Tell me what you've done today,' Mum said.

Keene clapped his hands to his mouth.

'What?'

'I drew you a picture. I forgot it downstairs. I'll get it.'

'No, Keene …'

Keene, in the process of sliding from the bed, stopped.

'You stay with me. You can show it to me later.'

'All right.'

'What have you done today?'

'I played with Bunch.'

Mum coughed. 'Where did you play with Bunch?'

'Outside.'

'Outside? How're my roses?'

Keene lowered his head. 'They don't look very good anymore.'

'It's been a long time since we took care of them.'

'Maybe we need some new flowers.'

'We could get some new flowers, but I'm sure we could still help the roses.'

'They're very wild.' Keene remembered the way they'd grown all over the spindles. 'I was going to prune them but I didn't know how.'

'Of course you know how.'

'Not without you.'

Mum patted his leg. 'All it takes is a bit of love, care, and attention.'

'I'll make a mistake.'

'That's okay.'

'What if I mess up?'

'I've told you before, it's okay to make mistakes. We all make mistakes. The important thing is that we learn. Okay?'

Keene nodded.

'What else did you do outside?' Mum asked.

'I saw a spider!'

'A spider?'

'Uh huh!'

'In my roses?'

Keene nodded again.

'The nerve of it.'

'All baby spiders came out of it.'

The bridge of Mum's nose crinkled.

'They climbed all over the big spider! Maybe they'll live in your roses, Mum. Can spiders do that? They might have a city there.'

Mum laughed. 'You have such an imagination, Kee,' she said.

'I was going to kill it.'

'Why?'

'Dad would've killed it.'

'It's just trying to live, like the rest of us. You don't have to be scared.' Mum brushed his cheek. 'You're my hero. My little superhero. Aren't you?'

Keene straightened and squared his shoulders.

'All we need is to get you a cape.'

Keene smirked sheepishly.

'What about your piano?'

'I don't play much.'

'Why not?'

'I don't want to wake you.'

'You can play whenever you want, Kee. I want you to. Okay?'

'Okay.'

'Now tell me about the rest of your day.'

Keene began haltingly, but her smile encouraged him and, as rain drummed the roof, lightning flashed and thunder rumbled, talking came easier. She hung onto his every word. Really, she hadn't changed that much.

When she yawned, he knew she'd nap again. She napped a lot now. He lay against her and pressed his cheek against hers. Her skin was cold and pasty and her arms were broomsticks, but as her hands clamped his back, he felt warm and safe. He missed that.

'Kee?' Dad said, as he clomped into the room.

Keene pulled himself free and Dad guided him from the bed. Averil swayed by the window, looking this way and that, like she didn't know where to focus. She got like that a lot now.

'We'll talk later,' Mum said.

'Okay, Mum.' Dad picked Keene up, so he could kiss her on the cheek. 'Love you.'

'Love you, too.'

'Kee,' Dad set him down, 'take Bunch and go watch some television.'

'Okay, Dad.'

Lightning lit up the room and, fleetingly, a shadow, tall and sinewy rose in the corner, then was gone.

Keene, in the act of turning, stopped.

'Kee?' Dad said. '*Keene.*'

'I'm going, Dad.'

Keene left the room as Dad sat on the bedside. Bunch pushed himself to his feet, his head low, his ears bent. Dad took Mum's hand between his own and rubbed it. She smiled. Keene waved back to her. Her smile broadened at him.

Dad got up and closed the door. As Keene was shut out onto the landing, something hit him – a sense of *wrongness*. He hugged Bunch. Bunch licked his face. Usually, Keene would've laughed. Now, he sniffled.

'I wish I had some way to help Mum,' he said. 'I'd do anything.'

He ran down the creaking stairs and stopped on the last step just as lights flashed on the screen door. Bunch sped past him and barked. The lights went out, a car door opened and closed, then footsteps shuffled onto the veranda. Bunch's tail wagged. Keene could smell food – he sniffed deeply, and decided it had to be roast chicken

Yvonne appeared in jeans and boots, a big woolly lemon-coloured jumper, and a brown Driza-Bone jacket. She shielded herself from the rain with one hand, and carried a basket in the other. Keene prodded the door open for her. Bunch sniffed at the basket.

'Thank you, sweetheart,' she said. 'Where's your dad?'

'He's upstairs with Mum.'

'Okay. How about you give me a hand in the kitchen? I brought dinner.'

Yvonne kicked off her shoes at the door, then led Keene and Bunch into the kitchen. She switched on the lights and put her basket on the kitchen table, then grabbed plates from the cupboard. She set three places, the chicken she'd brought, salad, and drinks – juice for herself and Keene and a beer for Dad.

'Come, sit down,' she said as she took a seat at the table.

Keene climbed onto the chair opposite her. Bunch sat on the floor under his dangling feet. The chicken *did* smell good and the skin was browned and roasted. Keene wasn't so sure about the salad; the lettuce and cucumbers reminded him of grass, and the tomatoes were big and squishy.

'Chicken's okay, isn't it?' Yvonne asked. 'I seem to remember you had seconds last week.'

Keene nodded. Yvonne's pale face was freckled. He wondered what sort of picture would emerge if he connected all her freckles. Maybe there'd be no picture but just wrinkly lines, like she might have if she was one-thousand-years old. He bent to rub Bunch behind the ears. Bunch sniffed at Keene's hand.

'You really shouldn't have Bunch at the dinner table,' Yvonne said.

'But he's my friend.'

'He might be, but he's also full of germs.'

'He's not full of germs!'

'Keene, I like Bunch, too.' Yvonne scratched Bunch behind the ears. He lifted his head and leaned into Yvonne's attention. 'But he's still a dog and not as clean as us.' She went and rinsed her hands at the kitchen sink. 'Maybe you should wash your hands, too.'

Keene braced himself on his chair, but Yvonne was unflinching. She would wait now. And if he didn't do as he was told, she would wait until Dad arrived and ordered him.

He got down from his chair and rinsed his hands in the kitchen sink. Bunch followed and sat behind him.

'Have you had a good day?' Yvonne said.

'It was okay.'

'Just okay?'

Keene shrugged. He wiped his hands on a tea towel and stopped by the fridge. 'Can I have some chocolate?'

'It'll ruin your dinner.'

'Just a little?' Keene opened the fridge and took out a block of dark chocolate.

'Keene.'

Keene held the chocolate in his hands.

'Put it back.'

Keene's hands tightened around the chocolate.

'Please, Keene. Now.'

Keene put the chocolate back in the fridge and closed the door.

'I've got my eye on you, Keene.' Yvonne pointed at her eye, at him, then winked.

Keene sat back at the kitchen table; Bunch curled up on the floor.

'How about we start?' Yvonne said. 'Your dad can join us when he's ready.'

Keene peeled the skin from his chicken. 'Why do you always bring us food?'

'I'm just trying to help,' Yvonne said. 'That's what good neighbours do.'

She reached across to his plate with her knife and fork. He frowned and she pulled back. Keene tore off a sliver of chicken, ate half, then held the rest out for Bunch. Bunch wolfed it down, his teeth snapping.

'Keene, honey, we can feed Bunch after we've eaten.'

'Where's Ashley?'

'She's staying with her father this week.'

Keene tore some more meat from his drumstick.

'Do you like when I bring her?'

Keene shrugged.

'She likes to play with you.'

Keene lifted his meat to his mouth.

'You could come to my house and play with her. Would you like that?'

Keene shrugged again. The last thing he wanted to do was go to Yvonne's house.

'She'd like that. She says when you both grow up, she's going to marry you.'

Keene scowled. Yvonne smiled, and when Keene's scowl deepened, she lifted a finger to her mouth and her smile disappeared, although Keene could tell she was still trying to be playful. He bit into his meat and tore a chunk out of the chicken. Bunch sniffed at his elbow. Keene fed him a sliver.

'Keene, what did I say about feeding Bunch?'

'He's hungry.'

'He can wait.'

Keene bit down on a response.

'Ashley's having a birthday soon. Would you like to come?'

Keene tore some chicken from his drumstick. Footsteps tramped down the stairwell. Keene peeked at Yvonne, then held the chicken out towards Bunch.

'Keene!' It was Dad, coming down the hall. 'Don't feed Bunch until you've eaten. You've been told.'

Yvonne rose to greet Dad. They exchanged a brief embrace and kiss on the cheek. When they broke apart, Yvonne frowned at the loose strap on Dad's overalls, then squinted at where it had torn free.

'Do you want me to sew that?' she asked.

Keene gritted his teeth – that was something Mum did.

'It'll be fine,' Dad said, gesturing that they should sit down. He surveyed the dinner. 'This looks great, Yvonne. Thanks for this.'

'It's nothing.'

'How was the drive?'

'It's difficult out there.'

Keene focused on his chicken as they chatted, but Dad wouldn't let him go until he'd finished, so Keene ravaged his drumstick to the bone, and, when he was given a choice of eating his salad or a second piece, took a breast and raced through that, sneaking bits to Bunch when nobody was watching.

'You're certainly eating quickly,' Yvonne said.

Keene pushed his way clear from the table. He'd just hopped down from his chair when Averil entered.

'Is everything all right?' Dad asked.

'Deidre woke.'

Dad started to rise.

'She's back asleep now. But she was looking for a pendant.'

'A pendant?'

'A citrine pendant – do you know anything about that?'

'Is that the one I bought?' Keene said.

Dad nodded. 'From the school fair.'

'She wanted it with … her,' Averil said. 'I'm not sure … she wasn't entirely clear.'

'We lost it,' Dad said. 'Before she got sick.'

'Oh. Well, I'll just see that she's comfortable and settles back in for the night, then I'll be going.'

'Thanks, Averil. You're as watchful as an owl.'

'I'll be back first thing.'

'You're welcome to stay the night. We have only the couch, but it unfolds into a bed, and it'll save you a drive.'

'I'll see how things go. Excuse me.' Averil headed back through the hall and noiselessly up the stairs.

'Dad?'

Dad looked at Keene.

'Can we look for the pendant?'

'It's lost, Kee.'

'Maybe we can find it.'

'Kee, it's impossible.'

'But we have to look!'

'*Kee.*'

'We won't know until we—'

'Keene!' Dad glared at him.

Keene lowered his head and fidgeted. Outside, the rain hammered away. Yvonne reached across the table and clasped Dad's hand.

'Averil said Mum asked about your piano,' Dad said. 'How about you go play for a bit?'

'Okay, Dad. Come on, Bunch.'

Keene trundled from the kitchen and into the dining room, Bunch behind him.

Storm

Stomping over to the piano, Keene grabbed his picture and pencils, and dumped them on the coffee table. Tomorrow, he would show his picture to Mum and have Averil tape it on the wall alongside the others. Bunch leaped onto the couch, circled, and curled into a ball.

Keene hauled the roof tile onto the practice pedal, then scrambled onto the piano stool. Sheet music rested on the top of the piano beside an ornate red vase. He flicked through it and found Mozart's Piano Sonata 16 – a piece he'd practised often, but hadn't touched in months – and put it on the music desk.

His playing stumbled, and sometimes he hit keys too hard, but the music's flow encouraged him. He rocked on the piano stool as a coldness wove around him. This wasn't right. Mum was meant to be sitting next to him. She should have her arm around him. They should be moving together in rhythm with the music.

He dragged his hands clear as the last note tapered away and hushed voices drifted through the archway connecting the dining room to the kitchen.

'… have to go easy,' Yvonne was saying.

'He's fine,' Dad said.

'The look you gave him could've withered the bark from a tree,' Yvonne said.

'He's stronger than you realise.'

Keene could hear Dad get up and move. The radio came on – again, that hard rock music that he loved so much, and which he used to listen to so loud that Mum would shout at him to turn it down. Now he kept the volume soft.

'What is with you and this damned radio?' Yvonne said.

'It fills the emptiness, okay?'

'The house isn't empty. Keene is here. I'm here. And so is Deidre.'

'Then it fills the silence … '

'The silence – what are you talking about?'

'Just the way things used to be,' Dad's voice wavered, 'and the way things are. It's not the way things should be.'

A chair slid back. Then movement. Keene peeked through the archway. Yvonne hugged Dad. Dad pulled back and looked at Yvonne, his eyes soft. Keene gritted his teeth. None of this was right. But it could be, if he could find the pendant.

The vase on top of the piano peered down at him, like a piggy-bank that contained a secret treasure. Keene climbed onto the stool, teetered, but managed to grab the vase. Hopping from the stool, he upended the vase; coins clattered onto the hardwood floor, but no pendant.

He rifled through the piano stool, television cabinet, and the coffee table's drawers, pulled the cushions from the couch, then checked under the couch. Bunch watched him curiously.

When Keene was done with the dining room, he scoured the living room, then headed upstairs, Bunch trailing behind him. Keene stopped in front of Mum's room. The door was closed; she would be asleep. The pendant wouldn't be in her room, since they'd only moved her in there *after* the pendant had been lost.

He continued to his mum and dad's bedroom and ransacked drawers and closets and searched under the bed, then went into their bathroom and delved into the cupboards under the sink where they kept the towels. He unfurled each towel and laid them across the floor. Bunch, sitting in the doorway, watched him, tail swishing.

Above the bath was the medicine cabinet. Keene climbed onto the bath's rim, and was so intent on struggling for balance that he didn't hear the repeated heavy creaking on the stairs that could only mean one particular person was coming up.

'Keene!' Dad seized him by the armpits and planted him on the floor. 'What have you done?'

'I'm looking for Mum's pendant, Dad!'

'You've made a mess of the house.'

'I'm sorry.'

'Sorry?'

'I'll clean—'

'I think maybe it's best you went to bed.'

'But I haven't finished looking.'

'Keene!'

Keene slumped towards the door.

'Keene, toilet first.'

'But I don't need to.'

'Now, Keene. And brush your teeth also.'

Keene went to the toilet, then brushed his teeth as Dad towered over him. When Keene was done, Dad escorted him to his bedroom. Keene undressed and got into his pyjamas. Bunch sat in one corner, muzzle on his paws.

'It's not fair,' Keene said, as he struggled with the buttons to his pyjamas. 'We should be looking.'

'Kee, it's gone, okay?'

'It'll make Mum better.'

'What?'

'The lady who sold it said that crystals help people feel better.'

'I wish that were the case, Kee.' Dad kneeled before Keene and buttoned up his pyjamas.

'It can help, Dad!'

Keene got into bed and flipped onto his side as Dad drew the covers up.

'Dad?'

Dad turned away and made a sound – a hiccup maybe.

'*Dad?*'

'We've talked about this, Kee.'

'Mum's not going to die! She can get better.'

'Some things you don't get better from.'

'Why?'

Dad sat on the bedside. 'This illness … it's like a darkness inside her.'

'How did it get there?'

'It's just something that happens.'

'Maybe somebody gave it to her, like when Bunch ate that stuff from the garden and couldn't stop vomiting.'

'No, Kee, it's … it's … Kee. Keene. We've tried everything.'

Keene yawned, and stretched his arms. 'Not everything.'

'Yes, Kee. *Everything.*'

Keene grabbed Dad's hand. 'It'll be all right, Dad.'

Dad's smile was tired. 'No more tearing the house up, okay?'

Keene tried to come up with ways to avoid agreeing.

'It's not here, Keene. I think we lost it that Sunday we had the picnic at Miller's Pond. Remember that day it was so hot?'

Summer had been mild, except for one blistering weekend. They'd hiked to Miller's Pond. Mum rarely swam. Usually, it was Keene and Dad. And Bunch. Dad would throw the tennis ball around and Bunch would swim out and get it. But this time Mum had surprised them by stripping down to her one-piece. None of them had even known she was wearing it.

'Do you remember?'

Keene nodded furiously.

'The next morning was when … when your mum realised something might be wrong. That's when we started seeing lots of doctors. We forgot about the pendant. Whatever happened to it, it's gone. Okay?'

Keene didn't want to give up.

'*Okay?*'

'Okay, Dad. Will you read me a story?'

Keene grabbed a book – a collection of fairy-tales – from the pile on his bedside table. He flicked through *Little Red Riding Hood*, pausing briefly on Red Riding Hood confronting the wolf in Grandma's clothing; past *Sleeping Beauty*, where the Princess slept on her bed; and to a bookmark halfway through *Hansel and Gretel*, with the children in the house of the witch.

Dad closed the book and put it back on the bedside table. 'Not tonight, Keene.'

'Aw.'

'Please, Kee. Go to sleep. You going to be okay with the storm?'

Keene snuggled back into his bed.

'You know it's *just* a storm. Just thunder and lightning. You're a big boy now. You tell yourself to stay calm.'

'I will.'

Dad stroked his forehead. 'Night, Kee.'

'Night, Dad.'

Dad glanced at Bunch. 'You coming?'

Bunch lifted his muzzle. His tail whacked the floor twice. Then he rested his muzzle back onto his paws.

'Okay. Night, you two.'

Dad switched off the light and left the room. His footsteps were quiet across the hall but, as always, the stairwell creaked. Moments later, dim light flickered from under the crack of the door – the television – and Keene could hear Dad and Yvonne tidying up. Keene thought about getting out of bed to help. He *was* responsible. He rolled onto his side as lightning lit up the window and silhouetted branches grew into claws. Thunder shook the room. Wind howled until the weatherboards rattled. The room lit up once more. Shadows scraped at the window and leaves rustled. Then thunder. Keene listened to the rain thump on the roof until it receded into a steady drone, thinning to silence.

Now there was nothing but a pinpoint of white light that expanded, filling the room until the sun shone through the branches of Myrtle Beech trees, standing so tall and straight. Sweat beaded on Keene's forehead. Mum kneeled by him.

Bunch barked. Dad waded knee-deep into Miller's Pond, wearing nothing but shorts, his skin bronzed, a bright green tennis ball held aloft. Bunch pranced on the bank. Dad threw the ball. Bunch sailed into the water. Dad grinned, then dived after Bunch.

Mum fitted floaties onto Keene's arms, although he complained he could swim just fine. Then she unbuttoned her dress. It slid down her shoulders and bundled around her ankles. Underneath, she wore a one-piece, red swimsuit. She threw her head back. Her blonde hair was a stream of liquid gold.

The pendant – hanging on a fraying leather cord – sat framed beneath her collarbone, right over her heart, a citrine teardrop about to spill down her chest.

Mum undid the clasp. 'Just so I don't lose it,' she said. 'I'll have to get a proper chain for it.'

She refastened the clasp. The Candlebark that provided them shade had many low branches, its bark stripped white. Mum hung the leather cord over a thick, forked branch. The pendant flared in the sunlight every time it swung to the right.

'Let's go!'

She took his hand and led him to the bank of Miller's Pond. It wasn't really a pond, but a broad shimmering lake. Bunch panted, his tennis ball floating in front of him. Dad had been doing the backstroke, but he paused to float and admire Mum.

Keene stared at his reflection in the water. Dad whistled. Bunch picked up his ball and leaped in.

The surface of the water shattered.

Keene woke to a blinding white light as a branch from the gum tree crashed through the window. He screamed and Bunch leaped up and howled, but they were eclipsed by thunder rumbling through the house.

The bedroom door flung open and Dad bolted in and scooped up Keene. The branch filled the window and sprawled across the bed, still attached to the tree outside. Bunch barked and barked at the branch. Dad carried Keene out onto the landing – Bunch close behind – and slammed the door shut.

'Are you all right?' Dad said. He patted Keene over, as if looking for any injury. 'Are you hurt?'

Keene shook his head.

'Are you sure?'

Keene nodded. 'What happened?'

'I don't know. I think lightning must've hit the tree.'

The door to Dad's bedroom was ajar, the lamp on. Keene thought he could even hear rock music coming from Dad's clock radio, although it was so soft he might've been imagining it. Then it stopped.

'Can I sleep with you, Dad?' Keene said.

'With me?'

Keene nodded.

'Nolan?'

It was Mum's voice, strong and clear through the tumult of the storm.

Mum's door squealed as Dad opened it. They stepped into her bedroom. The shadows shifted in the night. Mum was just a silhouette in bed. Keene's attention strayed to the corner, but it was too dark to make anything out. Bunch waited in the doorway, panting.

'What's happened?'

Dad sat on her bedside, balancing Keene on his lap. Keene relaxed as Mum's face came into view, although it was pale and ghostly. Keene bit his lip. Her eyes brimmed and she smiled. It was her. Of course it would be.

'I think lightning hit the tree outside,' Dad said. 'It crashed into Keene's room.'

Mum caressed Keene's cheek. Her fingertips were so warm Keene imagined they glowed. 'Are you all right, sweetheart?' she asked.

He nodded.

'How about you stay with me tonight?'

'Really?'

'Maybe that's not such a good idea,' Dad said.

But Keene was already prying himself from Dad's lap and slipping under the covers of the bed, alongside Mum, into her warmth, and away from whatever shadows lurked in the corner. He felt the stiffness of her arms and the xylophone of her ribs, but it was safe here.

'He'll be okay,' Mum said.

'Are you sure?' Dad said, but he was already pulling the covers up.

'It's just like old times. Right, Kee?'

Keene's gaze fell onto her bare chest. It made sense now. She'd gotten ill the moment she'd lost the pendant. If he could get it back, things would be fine. He could tell them that, even tell them he remembered where it was, but it would be much better to surprise them.

As Mum and Dad exchanged goodnights, Keene began to plot how he would recover the pendant.

Tree

Keene blinked, trying to work out what had woken him. His body was frozen – only his eyes could flit around to take everything in. The room was shifting splashes of grey. Even his pictures on the wall had lost their colour, their details ugly smears, the collage forming the image of a dark shadow reaching out to grab him. Next to Keene, Mum's breathing was like a slow heartbeat, each inhalation coarse.

Lightning filled the room – all but the corner, where it was swallowed into an inescapable abyss. Keene *felt* it now and tried to scream a warning. Shadows rose around him, twirling up like plumes of smoke. A face appeared in the corner, skeletal, wispy, and grinning, shrouded in a cowl of midnight.

Sleeves reached out, hands emerging from the cuffs, thin and gnarled. Fingers walked up Keene's torso, leaving a contrail of icy fingerprints. The breath froze in his lungs as he tried again to cry out. The grinning shadow pulled the cover from his body while the others hissed, a discordant chorus that shook the bed.

'You …' it said, its voice a bitter wind that chilled his skin.

Mouth open, eyes depthless, lips pursed, it planted its hands on either side of Keene's shoulders. Keene's breath misted and a chill coated his skin. The hissing grew louder. The shadow flitted over to Mum and embraced her, its figure pulsating as it sucked the warmth from her body.

A scream built in Keene's stomach. Bunch whined outside the bedroom door, his nails restless on the floorboards, the silhouette of his movement flickering under the crack of the door. Keene needed to shout, to rouse Dad. He opened his mouth.

And gasped as he sprang into a sitting position. The night shredded into a grey morning that flooded the room. The shadows and darkness evaporated. He'd been dreaming – although the cover was pulled from his body. He doubted now that he had been sleeping. He'd seen something – the darkness that was hurting Mum. Her arm curled towards him and her chest rose and fell gently. Keene looked at her pursed lips and imagined he could see her breath, shallow and thin. He was tempted to wake her to make sure she was okay, but Averil came in to change the bag attached to the pole.

'Hello, sleepyhead,' she said. 'Better keep it down and let your mum sleep.'

Voices and thumping drifted in from outside. Keene checked the corner. Empty. But the shadows would come. He was sure of it.

'Maybe you should get yourself some breakfast,' Averil said.

'Okay.'

Keene pecked Mum on the cheek, then left the room. Bunch, waiting on the landing, rose, and licked Keene on the cheek as Keene hugged him.

'Come on, Bunch.'

Keene tiptoed down the stairs, trying to avoid the creaks, but as he got to the bottom, he heard sounds bustling through the screen door.

Bunch's ears pricked back and his tail straightened. Scuttling around in the yard were burly men dressed in blue overalls and bright lime vests, some gesturing to something out of Keene's sight, while others chatted. Two white trucks were parked in the yard behind them.

Bunch barked once.

'Sshhh, Bunch!'

Bunch growled.

'Sshhh! You stay.'

Bunch wagged his tail once.

'Stay!'

Keene pushed the screen door open, stepped onto the veranda, and gasped. The tree in the yard had been shorn in two. The stump was a charred stalagmite, taller than the men around it, the rest of the tree pitched against the house, only a sinew of trunk connecting the two. One of the workers – young, with a sparkling stud in his right ear – cut at the sinew with a saw, while others fastened ropes around the tree's trunk.

Mouth hanging open, Keene walked onto the grass. It was wet under his bare feet, and moisture oozed between his toes. The tree's outstretched branches embraced the roof, leaning on the house for support – all but the one branch that had impaled his window.

Backpedalling to get a good view of the house, his heel struck something – the tyre swing lying in the grass, its rope slack and coiled, still attached to the splintered branch to which it had been tied. It seemed unreal now, neither a tyre without a car, nor a swing without a tree. One end of the hammock had also shorn clear and it slumped around the roots of the misshapen gum.

Dad's agitated voice filtered through the other chatter, just loud enough to be heard, but not understood. He and a small plump woman dressed in a suit and oversized glasses, her hair tied into a bun, stood in front of a red car parked behind Dad's van, Yvonne's truck, and Averil's bug.

The woman shook her head.

Dad's right fist clenched, his voice rising. ' … been able to work because of my wife's cancer,' he was saying. 'This is unfair, Miss Whelan.'

'I'm sorry, but you're overdue. If you can't meet the pay—'

'Just go, okay? I can't deal with this today. I have enough to think about.'

'Mr. Hayes—!'

'I don't want to hear it!' Dad turned his back on her. 'Keene! What're you doing? Get back in the house.'

Dad strode toward him, so Keene began to jog backwards. The woman had opened her mouth, like she was going to say something to Dad, but when she saw Keene she grew pale. Keene frowned at her. Dad looked back, and now his anger fumed. He thrust a finger at Miss Whelan.

'That's right!' he said. 'There's a family living here! We're not just numbers – we're a family!'

'I'm sorry,' Miss Whelan said, and now her voice wavered. 'I'm just doing what I'm told.'

'And what you're told is to chase us out of here. You're nothing but a pack of wild dogs.' Dad put a hand on Keene's shoulder. 'Regardless of circumstances, regardless of who it hurts.'

Miss Whelan looked at Keene again, and whatever resolve held her up broke. She opened the door to her car and got in. Dad turned, and urged Keene back toward the house.

'Who's that, Dad?'

'Just a woman from the bank.'

'What does she want?'

Dad snorted. 'What doesn't she want?'

Keene frowned, not understanding. He hopped up onto the veranda.

'You're going to catch a cold walking barefoot in the grass,' Dad said.

'Dad, are these men going to fix the tree?' Keene asked.

'No. It has to come down.'

'It can't come down! They have to fix it.'

'Kee, the tree's ruined.' Dad opened the screen door and kicked off his shoes. Bunch trotted after them as they headed down the hall.

'Why?'

'It just is, Kee. Some things you can't fix.'

Yvonne was in the kitchen, cutting a sandwich. Keene climbed onto a kitchen chair and Dad poured Corn Flakes into a bowl. Yvonne's hair was tied in a loose ponytail, which made her almost girlish, and she was wearing the same clothes as yesterday.

'You're here early,' Keene said.

'I'm making you a sandwich.' Yvonne wrapped the sandwich and popped it into the fridge.

'For lunch, okay, Kee?' Dad placed the bowl of Corn Flakes and a glass of apple juice on the table, then turned the radio on. Even with the volume low, blaring guitars and thumping drums filled the kitchen. 'There's a lot going on,' Dad went on, 'so don't get in the way of the people working outside.'

'Okay, Dad.' Keene bit back on a smile and studied the way the Corn Flakes floated in his bowl. Staying out of sight would suit him perfectly.

'And don't go in your room until we do something about that tree. We've swept up a bit but there's still a lot to do. Keep yourself busy.'

'Busy.' Keene nodded.

'Just make sure I can find you if I need you.'

Keene froze in the act of lifting his spoon to his mouth.

'Understand?'

Keene nodded again. He'd have to risk it. He'd just have to sneak out and be back before anybody missed him.

A knock sounded from the screen door. It barely seemed to open, or make a noise. Then footsteps shuffled down the hall.

'Hello!'

The voice boomed into the kitchen, as if it might herald a giant. But it was Doctor Ward who appeared – small and elderly, and moving like he was trying to be as unobtrusive as possible. Although his face was careworn and his scruffy hair white, his blue eyes hadn't dimmed with age, and reflected a peaceful wisdom he must've accumulated over a lifetime of treating patients. In his right hand, he carried a leather bag that might've been black once, but was now faded and filled with cracks.

'Nolan. Yvonne.' Bunch zipped up to him, wagging his tail. Doctor Ward scratched him behind the ears. 'Hello, Bunch!'

Doctor Ward tousled Keene's hair. His suit was a drab grey, threadbare at the shoulders, and his shirt chamomile, but his bow-tie – askew to the right, as if somebody had tried to spin it – was an oceanic blue.

'Keene, how're you?'

'Good, Doctor Ward.'

Doctor Ward smiled, the lines in his face smoothing out. But then he scowled at the radio. 'Still listening to this racket, Nolan?'

'You get used to it,' Dad said.

'Give me Dylan, Simon and Garfunkel, McLean, Baez … well, anybody – *anything* – but this.'

'I'll convert you yet.'

'No thanks.'

'I'll take you to see Deidre,' Dad said, escorting Doctor Ward from the kitchen.

Keene dug into his cereal as Dad and Doctor Ward traipsed upstairs. Yvonne remained by the fridge. She seemed different today – paler, her lower lip pursed.

'What?' Keene said.

Yvonne sat down at the table. 'Your dad told me that, last night, he tried to talk to you about your mum's illness.'

Keene froze in the act of lifting his spoon to his mouth.

'Your dad said you didn't fully understand.'

Keene shrugged one shoulder.

'There are many ways we can get sick – I bet you've had colds and tummy-aches and ear infections and all sort of things, right?'

Keene nodded once, slowly. The spoon still wavered in his hand.

'There are lots of things like that. Most times we get better – sometimes by ourselves, and sometimes we need medicine. But there's also other ways we can get sick where we're not strong enough to get better, and medicine can't help us the way we'd like. Does that make sense?'

Keene gritted his teeth. She was wrong! Mum *would* get better. He slammed his spoon back into his bowl. Milk splattered out, and drops sprayed onto the right side of Yvonne's face. She flinched, then ran to the sink, keeping her right eye scrunched-up as she washed it out. Then she rose up straight, lifted her face to the ceiling, and pressed her middle finger to her eye. Slowly, she drew her finger back, keeping her fingertip carefully pointed up. Keene half-raised in his chair to try and see what she held there.

'What's that?' he said.

Yvonne absently grabbed the sponge with her free hand, then came over. She still held her other hand palm-up, her middle finger extended. On the fingertip sat a small glass disc.

'My contact lens,' she said.

'What?'

'They help me see, Keene. They're like the lenses in glasses, but I wear them on my eyes.'

'Do they hurt?'

'No, not at all.'

She curled her middle finger so that the lens fell into her palm, and closed her hand into a loose fist. She mopped up the milk spillage with the sponge.

'I want you to know,' she said, although her tone was flatter now, 'if I can ever do anything for you, you just have to ask.'

'Like what?'

Yvonne rose up, hands on her hips, right hand still closed into a fist. She might've been scary – the way Dad was, when he was unhappy – but her right eye was red and still half-squinted shut. Keene almost laughed, and had to fight hard to not smile.

'I need to clean my lens before I can put it back in,' she said, rinsing the sponge in the sink. 'But remember what I said.'

She swept from the kitchen, Keene bracing himself for the way she patted him on his head sometimes. But she didn't. He felt the air of her passing, then heard her footsteps go down the hall and up the stairs.

Yvonne was always nice to him, helping out around the house, bringing food, and sometimes cleaning up, but she didn't belong. She had her own family. Keene didn't know why she had to keep being here.

He finished his Corn Flakes and gulped down his apple juice, putting his empty bowl and glass in the sink. He was about to leave, but stopped, dragged a kitchen chair over, clambered onto it, and washed the plate and bowl, then slotted them into the dish rack. That would please Mum.

He climbed from the chair and pushed it back into the table. Rain sprinkled the window. It would make things harder, but that couldn't be helped. And like Dad said, it was only a storm – just thunder and lightning. He would have to brave it.

It was time he got going.

Warning

Keene hurtled up the stairs two at a time, then skittered to a halt. Bunch crashed into his legs and looked up, as if trying to work out what game they were playing.

The door to Mum's bedroom was ajar so Keene peeked in as he tiptoed past. Mum was asleep, Doctor Ward leaning over her, listening to her chest with his stethoscope. He'd let Keene listen once, Mum's heart as strong as the thump of a drum.

'Well?' Averil said.

'Is it …?' Dad said.

Doctor Ward took the plugs of his stethoscope from his ears as he straightened. 'It's a matter of time,' he said.

Keene hurried on.

The bedroom was dark since the fallen gum blocked the window. The branch that poked through stretched halfway across the room and lay on his bed like it was taking a nap, the bed sagging under its weight. The glass, splinters from the window frame, and leaves had been swept into a pile in the corner, although the branch must've shed more since others lay scattered across the floor.

Keene crept in and opened his closet. There had always been a staleness about the closet. Dad said it was because of the mothballs. Keene had never seen any moths shaped like balls, but wherever they hid, they sure stank.

He changed, took his raincoat from a hanger, and grabbed a pair of socks from one of the mesh drawers Mum had set up inside the closet. Then he scoured the room for his backpack – Bunch sniffing alongside him – and found it shoved under his bed among some toys.

Keene emptied the backpack of his school books and pencils, scattering them on the floor. He started to take his lunchbox out, but thought better of it. He unzipped the side pocket, found several chocolate wrappers, and threw them in the bin near his bedside table.

'Mind if I come in?'

It was the young worker with the saw. His boots were big and muddy, and a tattoo of what looked to be a snarling wolf's head sat on the left side of his neck. Bunch bared his teeth, a low growl rumbling in his throat. The worker held up his hacksaw and grinned.

'I'm here to cut the branch. Bet you'd like your room back.'

Bunch barked once.

'Hey, it's okay.' The worker held out his hand. Bunch craned forward and sniffed, then barked again.

'Sshhh, Bunch!' Keene said. 'Come on!'

Keene darted past the worker, flew down the stairs and back into the kitchen. He flung open the fridge door, grabbed the sandwich Yvonne had made, shoved it in his lunchbox – failing to clasp the lunchbox securely in his haste – and dropped it into his backpack, along with a bottle of juice, a bottle of water for Bunch, and a block of chocolate. He closed the fridge.

Bunch looked at him expectantly.

Keene opened the kitchen pantry, pushed aside cans of dog food, and hauled out a bag of dry dog food. He dipped his hand into the bag and examined the food he clawed out. Dad fed Bunch a handful, but Dad's hand was much bigger. Keene scooped both hands into the bag, but was still unsure. He dropped the dry food into his backpack, then followed it with two more double-handed scoops. Closing the bag he pushed it back onto the shelf and grabbed a box of dog biscuits, pouring several into his backpack. He put the box back and was about to close the pantry when he spotted a torch on the middle shelf. Dad used it to check outside whenever he heard a noise, although he only ever found animals rummaging through their garbage. One evening he used it to inspect the engine of his van after it had broken down. The torch was good for an emergency. Keene put it in his backpack and closed the pantry.

'Come on, Bunch!'

Keene lugged the backpack onto his back. It was heavy, dragging him off-balance, and rattled when he walked, like one of the maracas they handed out at school during Miss Klemke's music class. But he would carry it – he had to. This was important.

He started out the kitchen and into the hall, but saw Averil come in from the veranda. The screen door banged shut behind her. She started down the hall. Keene stopped, spun, and dashed through the archway that connected to the dining room. When he came back around to the hall, he peeked out and saw Averil go into the kitchen.

He tiptoed out, grabbed his shoes and yanked them on. Then he eased the screen door open, being slow and careful so it wouldn't screech. Doctor Ward's big brown Ford had just turned from the drive, and was heading down the road. Soon, it disappeared around the bend. The workers in the yard had tied ropes around the tree. Another time, Keene might've bothered them with questions. Now he wanted to get away.

He couldn't sprint across the yard – they'd see him – so he snuck across to the end of the veranda. The top of the balustrade was almost as high as his head. He took a step back, ran up, and leaped. He caught the balustrade, then scrambled – his feet running to gain purchase on the spindles – until he'd clambered over, falling more than landing in the drive by Dad's van. Bunch leaped up on the balustrade, balanced on his front paws, fell back onto all fours and poked his head between the spindles. He tried to push through, then took the long way, running down the veranda stairs and appearing in the drive.

'Good boy!' Keene said.

The rain grew heavier, so he wrestled the hood from his jacket. He scrambled past Dad's van, then across to Yvonne's ute, using the cars to shield him from the workers. He sprang up, and peeked out. The workers were still busy with the tree, so he stole his way behind Averil's bug. One worker turned back. Keene ducked, and looked at the line of trees.

It wasn't too far. One good charge would do it. He peeked around the corner of Averil's bug. The workers drew the ropes taut as lightning spider-webbed across the sky, like it was trying to entrap the last vestiges of the morning.

Keene burst from his cover and rode a surge of thunder across what remained of the yard. He pressed his back flat against the big, ugly gum tree. Bunch skidded to a halt, trying to work out where this game was going. Keene grabbed him by the collar.

'Come on, Bunchy! We have to hide!'

Bunch sprang forward so sharply that Keene fell onto his backside. Keene giggled as Bunch licked at his face.

'Stop it, Bunch!' Keene said.

He slid his backpack free and fished out a biscuit. Bunch snatched it from his palm. Keene scratched Bunch behind the ears.

'Good boy!'

Keene pushed himself into a kneeling position. The knees and backside of his pants were already wet, and the damp seeped into his shoes. His hands were cold. He should've brought his mittens and thought about going back for them. He peeped around the tree trunk. The workers had dropped their ropes and were talking. No – too risky.

Lightning flashed above the house. Thunder followed, so loud that the storm might've cracked the world open. The workers, almost shapeless in the downpour, scurried for cover on the veranda.

They were so cowardly. There were times when it had rained and Mum had taken Keene out in the yard, holding him to her chest as she danced with him while Dad berated their foolishness from the safety of the veranda. Mum would laugh and say that it was only rain, and while Keene had understood – had understood instinctively – Dad never had. Of course, it was raining heavier now than it had then.

Keene slung his backpack around his shoulders. 'Come on, Bun—'

'Where are you going?'

The voice was deep and coarse. Lightning speared the sky and the trunk of the tree lit up, revealing the face Keene had seen yesterday. As thunder roared, the tree shook, and the contours of its face swelled in its trunk until it became big and defined and disapproving.

'You are not to go!'

Keene took one backward step. Then another.

'What are you?' he said.

'I am the Witherwisp. You are not to proceed. You are to stay.'

'But—'

'Do. Not. Go!'

'I have to!' Keene said.

'You. Must. Not!'

The tree's trunk cracked and ground as the tree leaned forward and the branches curled to seize Keene. The soil around the roots churned as the tree tried to wrest itself from the earth. The other gum trees quivered in agreement.

'Stop! Now!'

'Nooo!'

'Now!'

Keene stumbled. The weight of the backpack dragged him onto his backside. He scampered to his feet as the tree's branches blotted everything from view. Keene scurried away on hands and knees until he found his footing.

He bolted deeper into the bush and did not look back.

Lair

Keene ran and ran until the ground disappeared and he was flying through the air. He fell into something soft and springy, and lay there, stunned. Bunch's panicked barking – now sounding as if it was coming from somewhere up high – roused him. Keene wanted to tell him to be quiet, but nothing came out – his voice was trapped in the bottom of his stomach.

Slippery thin fingers wrapped around his wrists and snaked up his sleeves. Something was grabbing hold of him and tightening its grip. He shook himself loose and hauled himself up, his breath coming back in a wheeze. Reeds had tangled around his wrists and ankles. That's all it was. He had to keep calm.

He looked around and found he was in a ditch, three of the walls smooth, the fourth bulbous with slate, shaped almost like a man with one arm lowered and another raised. Half the head was covered in moss. A crevice extended into the earth between the feet. Streaks of quartz glittered in the slate, almost like an arrow pointing up.

Keene rubbed a bump on his temple, wiped the wet from his cheeks, and patted himself down, but could feel no other injury. Bunch, luckily, hadn't fallen in, but his paws dug into the edge as he barked and barked. But then his bark stretched into a snarl, his muzzle pulled back to bare his teeth, and his tail lifted straight into the air. Keene leaned towards the crevice. He could *feel* that something was inside there, just ready to spring out.

You …

Keene wasn't sure he heard it. It could've been the wind or just his imagination. He pitched his head towards the crevice, half-hoping he would hear something as confirmation, but also half-hoping he wouldn't. Mist streamed from his breath. A chill ran up his arms. His legs grew leaden. Something was in here with him – he was sure of that now.

He leaped for the wall behind him, but it was too smooth to find grip. He tried again but his hands slid down it. His breath grew short. The tendril of a shadow poured from the crevice, growing darker and longer as it snaked towards him. The reeds curled and stretched, reaching for him like skeletal fingers.

Bolting, he sprang over the reeds and the shadow and caught the slate. He scurried for handholds as he yanked himself halfway from the ditch, holding onto the moss. His backpack dragged at him and his soles slipped.

The ground opened beneath him as the shadow blackened, undulating toward his flailing feet. The darkness mocked him. It contained the shadow from Mum's room. Perhaps this was where it lived, or where it took refuge during the day. The reeds reached for him, becoming charcoal grey as they entwined his feet.

Keene's shoulders ached and his hands numbed. If this were any other time he would let go, drop down, and try again, but he couldn't fall into the shadow. It would get him and stop him from helping Mum. And if it didn't, the reeds would. They would hold him down for the shadow.

The shadow shot out and tried to snake around his ankle. Keene kicked. His right foot struck something that propelled him up – a slate hand had emerged from the wall. A thin slit in the moss mouthed the word, *Go*. The slate gnashed as an arm extended from the face of the wall to boost him up.

Keene slid over the edge of the ditch and spun around, sure something was following him. The ditch was silent, the slate in the wall unmoving, the crevice black but vacant, the reeds now still. Bunch nuzzled at his face. Keene waved him away.

'Hello?' he called into the ditch.

Nothing, but the gum trees shuddered, and the knots in their trunks shook and bulged until Keene was sure faces would emerge. He took a step back, his foot hitting the edge of the ditch. He almost slipped, and threw out his arms for balance. The trees stopped and were quiet.

Whatever the shadow was, it must've scared the Witherwisp and the other gum trees into trying to warn him. But what could be so frightening? Keene leaned forward further to peer into the ditch. If only he could see! Whenever he used to have bad dreams, Mum would come in and turn on the lamp. That's when it hit him. He slid his backpack down his arms and, from among Bunch's biscuits and dried food, plucked out the torch. The beam highlighted the slate body, but splayed across the darkness of the crevice. The torch wasn't bright enough.

A hiss echoed from the crevice. Keene jumped back. The shadow was angry he'd escaped. Bunch resumed barking. Keene tensed up as he waited. He didn't know how long it would wait, but he *knew* the shadow would come out – it would come out for him and Mum. He flicked off his torch, dumped it in his backpack, and slung the backpack around one shoulder.

'Come on, Bunch!'

They kept walking, sometimes jogging, the bush growing darker as the storm raged. Keene frowned at the unchanging gum trees. They were meant to be burnt. There'd been a fire last year. Fire-fighters had put it out. The path was easy to spot because it wound through the blackened trunks. Maybe everything had grown back.

Something faint shrilled. The skin on Keene's arms crawled all the way to his neck. Distant, but distinct, a howl rose up. Then another, and another, and another. They sounded like wild dogs.

A ghostly cry startled him. Standing on the branch of a gum was an owl. It was mostly white, its face a mask, its eyes large and dark. It hooted again, leaped from the tree and sailed over their heads.

Keene gasped. He'd only ever seen owls in books, and never in the bush before, although he heard birds all the time, and occasionally saw kookaburras. He didn't know owls lived here. Maybe that's what the other sounds had been. Maybe.

'Come on, Bunchy!' he said.

They hurried onwards.

Cottage

Keene tried to spot any familiar landmark that suggested he was going the right way. The rain danced across the leaves and the wind shrieked through the branches. He hugged his arms to his chest. This had been so easy when Dad had lead them, but now gum trees loomed so tall and large and the bush was so unrelentingly gloomy.

He stopped to catch his breath, frightened and alone, thinking maybe he should turn back. Bunch nuzzled at his hand – usually a sign he was hungry. Keene set down his backpack, took out a biscuit and held it out, but Bunch wandered away, sniffing.

'Bunch?'

Tail straight, ears flat, Bunch walked towards a light that somehow shone down through the branches. He looked up, tilted his head to the left, then back to the right, then barked once. Keene re-shouldered his backpack and hurried over to join him.

It was the smallest opening in the intertwining gums – perhaps a branch had broken, leaving this gap through which light crept. Droplets of rain sprinkled through a kaleidoscopic prism. Then something wet prodded Keene's hand – Bunch's cold nose, sniffing at the biscuit Keene still held. He fed Bunch the biscuit, then looked around disconsolately.

He wasn't sure which way to go, and the new fear that rose up was that he wasn't sure what direction to take if – and it was just an *if*, he told himself – he wanted to head back home. He took several steps one way, then back, then left, then right, when the smell hit him: something cooking – something thick and savoury like a stew. Dad had said nobody lived out here, but this was close.

'Bunch!' Keene called.

They ducked from tree to tree, until they arrived at a small clearing that contained a cottage made of large, rough stones. Its roof was thatched and the chimney trickled white smoke. Big square windows flanked a scratched wooden door with rusty hinges.

Keene crept up, rose onto his tiptoes, and peered through the window into a kitchenette with a black stove. Adjoining it was a dining room with a fireplace, the fire nothing but embers. Still, it looked warmer than being out here.

A hand closed on his shoulder. Keene spun, and pressed himself flat against the cottage.

A crone bent over him, her face shrouded in white hair, except for one red streak above her left temple. One eye glowered at him emerald green, but the other was sewn shut with a cross-stitch.

'Oi,' she said, 'what d'ya think you're doin', lookin' into me house?'

Keene tried to answer but the words stuck in his throat.

The crone kneeled so that her back and shoulders swelled within her suede coat, the material splotched, the trim lined outrageously with black fur. Her right hand – a claw with long, pointed nails painted black – remained on Keene's shoulder. Tucked under her left arm was firewood.

'Tell me now, boy,' she said.

'I'm … lost.'

The crone chuckled and pushed herself to her feet. She limped to the front door and swung it open. 'Come, boy. *Now*. I 'ave somethin' to tell ya.'

'To tell me?'

The crone nodded. 'About what'cha doin'.'

'You don't know what I'm doin'.'

'Don't I? Come. I don't mean you any 'arm. Your dog stays outside.' She disappeared into the cottage.

Keene peeked around the door jamb. Warmth caressed his face, and that smell that had first attracted him grew overpowering. The crone unloaded her wood into a brazier, all but one piece, which she dropped into the fireplace. She stirred the embers with a poker until flames shot up.

'Come or go, jus' close the door,' she said. 'You're lettin' the cold in.'

Keene patted Bunch on the head. Bunch licked his palm.

'Wait here, Bunch,' Keene said, stepping into the cottage.

He did not close the door all the way, planning to remain near enough that he could escape if needed. A crooked smile twisted the crone's lips. She strode towards him and planted her hand onto the door. It thumped shut.

'Warm yourself by the fire,' she said.

Keene raced through the cluttered kitchen. Ceramic bowls and plates sat on shelves and counters, and pans hung from a rack. A black tin pot boiled over the stove. Stretched across a shaggy rug in the dining room was a tattered couch. Keene thrust his hands out to the fireplace. Already, the wood was burning.

'Can I in'erest you in somethin' to eat?'

Keene's stomach grumbled. The crone was in the kitchen now, stirring her black pot. She grinned a smile too big for her face, her cheeks becoming pointed, her good eye thin.

'Well?'

Something hot would be perfect, but Keene was pushing his luck already. He shouldn't even be in here. And he shouldn't take food from strangers. He shook his head.

'Ya sure?' The crone scooped food from the pot into one of her ceramic bowls. 'Ya look 'ungry. Come 'ere.'

'What …?'

'Come. Now.'

The crone hunched at the head of the crude wooden table that sat in the kitchen. Keene gulped and joined her, clambering onto one of the chairs. She shoved in front of him a bowl that contained chunks of meat and vegetables – such as potatoes and carrots – all coated in a thick, brown sauce. It *did* smell good.

'Eat,' the crone said, taking the chair opposite him. 'Eat before it gets cold.'

Keene picked up his fork and dug at the food. One of the chunks in the bowl rolled in the sauce, then blinked open to reveal an eye. The pupil dilated. Keene gasped and jumped, his chair screeching across the floor.

'What's the matter, boy?' the crone said.

Keene held his fork aloft, ready to stab the eye but, now, it was just a small round potato. He prodded it. Nothing. He prodded it again, so it rolled over, then shaved away the sauce with the hem of the fork. Still nothing. The crone cackled.

'Eat up,' she said.

Keene set his fork down. 'I have to go.'

The crone seized Keene by the wrist, stooping in her chair so that her face was inches from his. Keene flailed but she was too strong. The crone's mouth drew into a thin, humourless smile.

'Ya know what's out there, don't ya?' she asked.

'Let me go!'

'IT *knows* about you.'

'IT? What is IT? Who is IT?'

'*You* know. IT takes many forms and has many faces. But *you've* seen IT. *You've* felt ITs cold breath. Do you really thin' you can stop IT? That you can turn IT back?'

'T–t–turn IT b–back?'

The crone slid from her chair, one knee pressed to the floor as her bony hand stroked Keene's cheek. 'You can't beat IT. You can *never* beat IT. You can only ever stall IT – for a little while, at least.' She traced the curve of his face with her fingernails. 'But IT knows you now and IT will stop you. IT has many friends, many allies, many faces. Go home.'

'No.'

'Go!'

'No!'

The crone threw her head back and laughed. 'Then be on your way!' She lifted her hands up above her head. 'Just 'member what I've told ya!'

Keene leaped for the door and grabbed the doorknob. The door rattled in its frame and he was afraid he wouldn't be able to get it open, but then it unlatched and swung wide. Cold air blasted him. Bunch barked, and spun in a circle.

'Come on, Bunch!'

Keene ran from the cottage, Bunch close on his heels.

Bridge

Everything was a shimmering green blur that closed in on Keene as he ran.

But he had to get away.

From the crone.

From IT.

He ran harder. But then the greenery faded into a charcoal black, the very colour leeching away. Leaves disappeared and the ground crunched underfoot. Keene stopped, hands on his thighs. Bunch ran back to his side to make sure nothing was wrong.

The leafless gum trees now were skeletons, tall and charred and twisted as if in pain, their gaunt branches entangled. Keene could hear them moaning, could feel their anguish, could see the way they writhed in agony. The ground was thick with soot and charcoal, and flecks of charcoal wafted in the rain.

Something small and as blue as flame shot up from within the roots of a nearby tree, like it was emerging from a bow to greet him – a small flower. It wasn't a rose. Keene would've recognised a rose. It might've been an orchid. Mum would love it – something new for the garden.

Keene let his backpack slide from his arms, then speared his hands into the soot. He shovelled it away until he reached moist earth. He dug around the flower, Bunch – whether understanding Keene's intent or simply mimicking – burrowing away with his nose.

'Careful, Bunch!'

It wasn't long before they'd dug a crater around the blue flower. Keene tugged and it came reluctantly – he was sure it quivered; or perhaps it had sighed – its roots dangling with mud. Bunch sniffed at it, trying to work out whether he could eat the prize of their labours.

'No, Bunch!'

Now Keene needed a way to take it home. He checked the side pocket in his backpack, but the orchid would probably get crushed in there. He opened the backpack. His lunchbox, standing on its side, stared back at him, its lid ajar, gaping at his intrusion.

Keene yanked out the lunchbox and tore it open. Yvonne's sandwich remained pristinely wrapped as neatly as any gift. He dumped it – the soot and mud on his hand smearing across the wrap – in the backpack.

The orchid fit perfectly in the lunchbox. Keene packed some soil around its roots, then held the lunchbox aloft to catch the rain. When there was enough in the lunchbox to keep the orchid happy, Keene carefully resealed the lid. He eased the lunchbox into his backpack.

Something hooted from the tree. Bunch leaped onto his hind legs, his paws against the trunk. It was the owl. Its wings fluttered once, then it swooped away.

'Come on, Bunch!' Keene said.

Although the owl soon disappeared, Keene ran until shafts of light shot through thinning gums. The trees fell away into a mist that made everything hazy – fog, at first glance, but on closer examination, spray from the overflowing river. The clouds were rolling grey hills that gnashed against one another.

Water crashed on the banks and lapped at Keene's shins. The bridge was nowhere to be seen. He needed to find the path. When he'd come here with Mum and Dad, they'd emerged from the path and there'd been the bridge.

He ranged ahead, but when he was sure he'd gone too far, doubled back – but with no luck. Maybe he was lost, although on the other side of the river everything was so familiar: gum trees huddled in the cold as they rose up over the hills, their peaks obscured in rumbling clouds. Keene had once called those hills 'mountains' – at least until Mum had corrected him. Miller's Pond was just over the first.

A growl filled Keene's ears. He took cover under a pyramid of two trees – one had fallen into the other. Bunch barked shrilly at the sky. The shadow that passed was dark but fleeting. IT was out! And looking for them! Just as the crone had warned him. And there was the path – winding into the darkness. The opening had been hidden by the fallen tree. Keene's grin faded. There still was no bridge opposite it.

He forced himself forward until his legs disappeared in the water. Perhaps he could swim. Another step. The torrent knocked him down and he rolled and bounced on something hard. He pushed himself up to find he was ankle-deep in the middle of the river.

He stamped his foot. The vibration echoed up his leg. The bridge was under the water. He'd found it! Bunch barked distantly.

Bunch!

Bunch ran up and down the bank, yapping. Every now and again he would poise to spring forward, but dig his paws into the mud and gawp, the way he did whenever they tried to get him into a bath at home.

'Come on, Bunchy!' Keene shouted, but the wind scattered his voice before it could reach the bank.

Bunch darted, span, and barked. Keene called and called but it was useless. Whining, Bunch lowered onto his front legs. Keene slid the backpack down one arm until he could reach into it and pull out a biscuit.

'Come on, Bunchy!'

Bunch barked.

'I'll eat it, Bunchy!' Keene put the biscuit to his mouth.

Keene's hand trembled. A boom rolled across the river into a thickening shadow that swept over him.

'Now, Bunchy! Please!'

Bunch sprung over the water and yelped when his paws struck the bridge. He bounded towards Keene. Keene thrust out the biscuit.

'Good b—!'

Keene saw the wave only fleetingly – a raging torrent of foam shaped like a face howling in glee. Then the water hammered him from his feet and flung Bunch through the air. Wet fur struck Keene's face and he fell to one knee. His arms shot out and he grasped for, but missed, Bunch's tail.

Bunch plummeted into the river and was swept away.

Wind

The wind billowed and howled until it screamed inside Keene's head. He leaped from the bridge and fell onto the muddy bank, lying there and crying as images of Bunch flashed through his mind. Mum had wanted him to have a friend so they'd driven to a breeder's farm. Bunch had been a portly puppy in a litter of eight who'd hogged the blankets in one corner and – as Mum had said – bunched himself up. Keene had lifted him and held him clumsily. Bunch's fur had been soft, his body warm, and he'd smelled of milk. When he licked Keene across the cheek, that had been the decider. Now he was gone. Dad would be furious; Mum would be devastated.

Keene crawled towards the quivering gum trees and had to fight to gain his feet. The wind whipped around him and knocked him down, like Ben Dawes – the bully at school – sometimes did during recess. Keene gritted his teeth, hauled himself back up, and ploughed onwards.

A path appeared behind some shrubs, leading to a jagged and rocky stairwell that wound up the hill. Bracken hung dishevelled to either side, thickening into shrubberies. Keene used them to pull himself up. A step beneath his foot crumbled. He fell, struck his knee; the cuff of his pants tore. He looked over his shoulder. A whirlwind of debris towered into the form of a reaper that wrenched trees from the earth.

Here IT was again.

IT didn't want him to succeed.

IT didn't want him to save Mum.

Keene hurried on, his line of vision racing up the hill, weaving through quaking shrubs. The crest was lost in an eddying mist. But, in front of him, a trellis of vines fluttered, revealing two granite slabs framing a dark, triangular opening. Keene dived into it and crawled until his backpack caught in the narrow shaft. He slid it off, just in time to see the gum trees splinter as IT barrelled through them.

Keene backed further into the darkness until the opening was a pinpoint. He hugged his knees to his chest. Poor Bunch was gone. Keene clenched his teeth, rested his head on his forearms, and rocked back and forth, trying to stop himself from crying. It was all his fault.

The storm receded until only darkness and stillness remained in the cave. Dad would be frantic; Mum would be waiting. Keene heard her music in his ears. It lulled him until a peacefulness overcame him, or maybe he slept. But then a single thought sparked in his mind.

Mum was *waiting!*

His head shot up. Something breathed behind him, then rumbled. He reached out and at first felt only emptiness, but he pawed around until his right hand closed onto something soft – fur. He ran his hand down and felt the contours of a warm body, felt the heartbeat. Something cold touched at the back of his hand and whiskers bristled against his skin.

'Bunch …?'

Keene rocked back onto his knees, felt his backpack at his legs. How stupid! He'd already made the same mistake once. He rifled through his backpack. Something got up beside him, followed by an inquisitive whine. It had to be Bunch! Bunch was back!

'Bunch!' Keene said.

His hand closed on the torch. He turned it on and yanked it out. A beam of light sliced through the cave and settled not on Bunch's deep brown eyes, but on a pair of angled golden eyes, a set of ears – growing pointed – and a shaggy crimson head.

Keene pushed himself back by the heels and waved the torch across the cave. Other golden eyes greeted him. Noses crinkled, sniffing. The one Keene had petted – the biggest – snarled and stepped forward.

Dingoes!

The torch fell from Keene's hand and went out. He scrambled for it, then scampered through the shaft, dragging his backpack after him, but expecting teeth to sink into his leg. He broke through the vines and rose before the granite slabs. Could he have imagined it? He leant forward. The opening remained dark and still. He pointed his unlit torch at it. His finger played on the switch. No, it was best left alone.

He slung his backpack over one shoulder, and hopped up the path. Wind lamented through the gum trees – at least those which remained standing. IT had cut a swath of devastation, obliterated trees, scattered branches, and cratered the earth. The rain grew heavier, pounding at Keene's face. He kept his head lowered and pushed on.

The mist was at first sparse, but as Keene went higher, it grew thicker and thicker, until it engulfed him. Now he could see nothing but his own hands trying to feel his way forward, and could trust only the hill beneath his feet. The sense of danger pressed at him.

He ran, frightened he would never be able to find his way out. But no sooner had he thought that than he rose above the mist, and arrived on the crest of the hill – a small, jagged clearing with a scattering of boulders. The clouds swirled just above him – so close that if he stood on his tiptoes, he could reach up and grab them. On the middle of the crest, the sun shot through a funnel that had opened and lit up a bright golden circle on the ground.

Keene bounded over and basked himself in the sun's warmth, and revelled in the openness of that single patch of blue sky.

He heard the patter of footsteps behind him and spun.

The dingoes glided up out of the mist and fanned out to face him.

Pond

Keene glanced back over his shoulder. Miller's Pond was just down the hill. If he could make it that far, he might be able to climb one of the trees around the pond, although it was unlikely he could outrun the dingoes.

The largest dingo bent its forelegs as it growled. The others snarled until they synchronised into a single chorus. Their golden eyes fixed on Keene. Keene rummaged through his backpack. His hand closed on one of Bunch's biscuits. He held the biscuit out.

The lead dingo sniffed, then howled. The others followed. Keene shuddered, reminded of the howling he'd heard earlier, although this was deeper, almost operatic. Another sound piped in from much further away – barking, shrill and almost playful. Then again, louder now.

A blur of black and white streamed up out of the mist – Bunch! He dashed through the dingoes and circled Keene, dropped to his forelegs and barked. His fur was wet and stuck to his body, making him look thin and sickly. His tail shot up; his ears – usually so floppy – pointed up.

The dingoes seemed unsure of how to respond. Bunch barked again and again, each bark becoming shriller. The lead dingo wailed. Bunch's bark melted into a quavering whine. The lead dingo flicked its head, almost dismissively, and walked back down into the mist. One by one, the other dingoes followed.

Bunch cavorted around Keene. Keene dropped to his knees and held his arms out wide.

'Bunch!'

Bunch shook the water from his coat, then hurled himself at Keene, knocked him to the ground and licked his face. Keene hugged him, unable to stop laughing. Bunch broke free, his nose cold on Keene's wrist. A moment later, he seized the biscuit from Keene's hand and crunched on it.

Keene scratched him behind the right ear. If only he had a towel to dry Bunch. Mum had always said it was important to dry him after a bath so he wouldn't catch a cold. He hadn't had a bath, but he *was* wet. Still, there was no option now but to sit in the sun.

Bunch would have to be bathed when they got home, though. How long would it take Mum to get better? Dad wouldn't want to be involved. Yvonne would offer to help the way she always did. Keene sighed as he pulled his sandwich out of his backpack. Maybe Yvonne wasn't so bad.

Keene ate half of his sandwich – now squashed and flat at one end – although he tore the ham that spilled from the seams of the bread and fed it to Bunch. He also fed Bunch three handfuls of his dry food, piling it in a mound, and followed it with a snack: four blocks of chocolate and a sip of juice for himself, and another biscuit and a sip of water – directly from the bottle – for Bunch.

Once they were done, Keene shouldered his backpack. 'Come on, Bunch.'

They crossed the crest and headed down the slope. Keene fumbled for Bunch, felt wet fur, and curled his fingers into Bunch's collar. Howls rose up from below and pierced the mist. Perhaps the dingoes had circled, although it didn't sound like them – now it was shrill. Maybe it was the other howlers. Bunch whimpered.

The dingoes hadn't scared Bunch – not really. But whatever this was, it did.

The slope was treacherous and slick as Keene sidestepped his way down. Bunch – wheezing against his collar – glanced back, ears bowed low against his head. Keene relaxed his grip but did not let go.

Shapes appeared – darkening silhouettes. The mist thinned into a tumultuous sea of black clouds that foamed and raged. Lightning crackled and thunder boomed. Bunch yowled and jerked.

Keene slipped and slid down the slope, rolling end over end. Thunder bellowed and filled every pore of him, every breath, and the blaze of lightning sheared him in two until he was disembodied and knew – just for a moment – nothing but Mum, lying in her bed, gasping, a skeletal hand gesturing for Averil while Dad stomped around the house, calling for him.

He landed in something feathery, his right hand closed around Bunch's collar, only Bunch's barking resounded from behind him, growing louder and nearer and more desperate until Bunch nuzzled at Keene's neck.

'Bunch …?'

Keene lifted his face. Tulips fluttered in the wind, but now they rose up straight and brightened into a luminous rainbow that streaked towards the pocket of tall, majestic Myrtle Beeches that surrounded the pond. Standing resolute amongst them, its branches and leaves huddled, was the Candlebark, although its white bark had dirtied into something grey. Beneath it, the once docile surface now turbulent, was Miller's Pond. The river gushed from it, hair-pinned between two shallow hills and wound from sight.

Keene held Bunch's collar out. 'Come on, Bunchy!'

Bunch poked his head through the collar, and lolled his tongue out.

They bound across the tulips, slowing only when they reached Miller's Pond, a quagmire that had flooded the grass and flowers and thickets that had once surrounded it. Now they floated aimlessly or bobbed, as though fighting for breath. It was impossible to believe that Mum and Dad had ever taken him swimming here or that there'd ever been sun, or laughter, or happiness.

The Candlebark rustled, leaves floating to the ground. Keene picked his way through the slush, recalling the way Mum had hung her pendant. He scoured the branches, jumped up and down, tried other vantage points, but there was neither sign of the pendant, nor the branch it had been hung upon.

He slumped against the trunk, half-kneeling and keeping his behind above the flooded bank, elbows planted in his thighs, chin rested on his hands. Twigs and plants floated across his path. Bunch nestled up to him and wagged his tail. Keene didn't pat him. This had been for nothing. That day had been so long ago. Somebody might've come along and taken the pendant, or perhaps the wind had blown it clear. They were done. IT had won.

Something fluttered above his head – the owl, settling on one of the branches and gazing at him. Keene brushed at tears. The owl hooted once, then again.

'What?' Keene said.

The owl hooted again.

'*What?*' Keene said.

The owl blinked and, with a beat of its wings, hopped onto a forked branch. Keene shot up. This forked branch had been above the branch Mum had hung her pendant on, but now that branch was gone, with only a stark wound in the trunk remaining.

Keene whizzed around the Candlebark. The branch's shorn end sat upright, its tip speared through a thicket that was mostly underwater now. He waded his way out to it, while Bunch barked his concern.

'It's all right, Bunch!'

Bunch wasn't assured.

Keene began a frantic search. No pendant hung from the end of the branch, nor was it tangled in the thicket's leaves. He checked again and then a third time, but to no avail. It had to be here somewhere.

Lightning blazed across the pond's rocky surface. Thunder followed; then, rising up until it hurt his ears, the wind wailed.

Shearing through the tulips was the enormous shadow, a whirlpool of darkness that spun up and twisted the clouds into an angry grimace.

IT had come for him.

Shadow

Keene's mouth dropped open and he staggered back. Bunch, whining, leaped into the water and paddled past him.

'Bunch! Wait—!'

Something gleamed from the bottom of the pond, half-embedded in the mud. Keene looked at the shadow as it marched towards him. There was still time. He dived down and tried to swim to the bottom, but his backpack floated up like ballast. Bunch, now bedraggled on the opposite bank, barked, telling him to hurry up.

The shadow tore a zigzag through the tulips and wrenched beeches from the earth, growing darker and larger as it neared. Keene plunged into the water. It was murky but he could see something floating up from the shiny object: a cord – just like the one the pendant had.

Keene stretched for it but could only brush it with his fingertips. He tried again but it swayed from reach. Bubbles spouted from his mouth. He propelled himself up and flicked wet hair from his face.

Beeches whirled through the sky as the shadow veered towards the pond, cutting a ravine across the bank. Keene plummeted back down, kicking and thrashing. Bubbles silhouetted his dive as his fingers hooked the cord and his knees hit the pond's muddy bed.

Something burst from the mud and flared, a minute explosion, like the eruption of a match-head – the pendant! His hand tightened around it, and he was sure he could see the pendant glow through his skin. After everything that had happened, after almost giving up, he had it!

Keene kneeled there and revelled in the moment of calm.

So quiet.

So peaceful.

But now, he had to get home.

He rose to the surface and into a fury of sound and sight. The shadow roared as it swallowed up the

Candlebark and catapulted it into the sky. Other beeches were shorn into an inferno of leaves and woodchips. Bunch's barking heightened to a yowl as he reared back

The pond spewed into the shadow's ravine and flooded into the river. A swell broke across Keene's back. He was tossed and dragged into the torrent. Kicking and paddling, he broke the surface and bobbed up onto his back, his backpack buoyant under him.

The sky shattered as lightning struck the bank, inches from Keene as he floated past. Bunch chased him but was unable to keep up, his bark fading until it could no longer be heard. Then the thunder, a rolling rumble that heralded a blinding downpour. Keene had no idea how long it went on – the only thought that possessed him now was he had to get home. He had to beat IT back. Hills blurred past, until they flattened into a quagmire of reeds and saplings, and the storm rained itself out.

The backpack hooked onto something and its straps cut into his shoulders. He kicked; his right heel struck something hard. He swung with his arms and his right hand felt something smooth but unyielding. He flipped himself in the water, his hands closing on the edge of a rectangular marble slab that poked just above the surface. His feet landed on something equally solid and he was able to kneel, then stand, water lapping at his thighs.

Lines of odd shapes surrounded him, only their heads apparent – rectangular slabs, curved facades, blocks, and shapes he couldn't identify. Rising up, bathed in sunlight trickling through the clouds, was a shallow hill. On the hill was a willow with a crooked trunk. Surrounding it were rows of other shapes lost in diffuse golden light that twinkled on the water.

The shadow veered around the hills as clouds funnelled around it and lightning crackled. Then the thunder again. But now Keene was unmoved. He clutched the pendant tighter. He had to get it to Mum.

'Bunch …' Keene said. 'Bunch!'

The shadow's scream tore through Keene's head. IT didn't want him to get home. IT didn't want anything but destruction and pain. That was how IT fed – Keene understood that now.

'*Bunchy …!*' he called.

Nothing.

Bunch would have to find him.

Keene shoved the pendant in his pocket. His hair whipped about his face and a breeze rustled down his collar. He took a step toward the hill, plunged into the water, and paddled his way across.

The shapes became clearer now – they were made from stone, dark and polished, and lettered in gold. Headstones! He was in the cemetery, which *was* all right. The cemetery was near the road. If he could find that, everything would be fine.

Keene lurched to the top of the hill, up to a freshly dug grave under the crooked willow. Water filled half of the grave. Its headstone was a pristine charcoal marble; the lettering across its face glowed. Keene traced each letter with his finger, mouthing the sounds he had learned in school.

'Dah … ehhh … eee … dah … rrrr … ehhh … Haaah … ahhh … yeh … ehhh … sss.'

He tried to form the first word, but it choked in his throat. The second word, the one beginning with 'H', was his surname – he recognised it from the way it was written on his schoolbooks. The first name remained unpronounceable, although it started with the same letter as Mum's.

He fell to one knee. This was Mum's grave. He choked back a sob. No, it couldn't be. She was alive – and she was going to get better. He ran his hand over the letters, as if that would erase them from the headstone. But they stayed fixed. He leaped to his feet. IT wouldn't get her.

He wouldn't let IT.

The shadow corkscrewed through the river. Keene dug the pendant out of his pocket, wrapped its cord around his hand, and held it in his closed fist as the shadow ploughed towards him, hurling aside headstones and chewing the ground into muddy gorges. Coffins bobbled up, some rotted, others polished; several spewed grinning skeletons in tattered clothing that bobbed past him.

The shadow screamed as IT twisted, as if IT was broken and attempting to straighten ITself out. The face Keene had seen in his dream appeared in the darkness and ITs arms unwound to grab him. Then nothing but the tumult: a storm of mud, water, and debris, and the shadow's all-encompassing roar.

IT bent towards him, ready to scoop him up.

You …

Keene thrust the pendant out, letting it dangle from his hand. 'Leave her alone!' he said, although he neither heard nor felt a single word from his mouth.

The pendant flared in the sunlight and the shadow recoiled, pulsed, then exploded into innumerable dark splotches that tumbled through the air, like kites bereft of wind. Keene was pitched towards the open grave. He screamed and flailed. The splotches hit the ground and scurried away on spindly legs, their bulbous bodies undulating, the chorus of their whines – the howls he'd heard when he first set off – trebling to agonising shrieks.

For an instant time jarred, and a screech filled the cemetery, shattering headstones, shredding the bush, and shaking the clouds apart to reveal dashes of light.

Then it was gone.

And with a splash, Keene landed in the grave.

Hope

Muddy water swallowed Keene, filled his mouth and his nose, and gurgled in his chest. His feet hit something soft – his first thought was that it must be his mother's coffin. He bounced off it and broke the surface of the water.

The pendant's cord was still wrapped around his hand, the little stone buried in muck. He rubbed it clean and held it aloft. It pulsed like a heartbeat, and he was sure its warmth seeped into his palm. The shadow was gone. The pendant had destroyed IT. Now he had to get home to help Mum. He just hoped there was still enough time.

If there wasn't …

It didn't bear thinking about. He stuck the pendant in his pocket and zipped it shut, then tried to climb out of the grave, but the walls were muddy and slick.

'Hello!' he said. 'Hello …? Bunch?'

Nothing.

Keene grimaced. 'Hel—?'

A face popped up at the top of the grave. 'Hello!'

It was the crone. She thrust a thin hand down.

'Here!' she said. 'Let me pull you up!'

Keene shook his head and backed away until he hit the end of the grave.

'Now, boy!'

'No!'

'I want to help you.'

'I don't believe—'

Bunch appeared alongside her, fur wet and dirty, tongue hanging from his mouth.

'Bunch …?'

Bunch barked once. Keene could imagine his tail wagging.

The crone thrust her hand forward again. 'Hurry!'

Keene closed his hands around the crone's. Her skin was warm, her knuckles sharp, the joints in her fingers knobby, but she hauled Keene up effortlessly. He scurried over the edge, then hugged Bunch. Bunch licked at his face. The crone watched, her face tired, her arm hanging limp.

'Go …'

Keene got up and scurried down the slope, feeling the crone's eye on him. She had helped him – despite what he had thought, despite the way he'd distrusted her at first, she had helped him when he needed it most. Once he accepted that, he understood that's all she had ever been trying to do.

As he reached the waterline, he waved once to her. 'Thank you,' he said.

The crone's lips twitched into a fleeting smile.

Keene plunged back into the water. Cold engulfed him and froze the breath in his lungs. The gum trees shimmied; their branches parted to offer glimpses of a road. Keene bounced on his tiptoes, but soon it was shallow enough that he and Bunch could walk, and then there was the earth, soaked and marshy but ground nonetheless.

Gum trees shuddered and embraced them. Faces were etched in their trunks – big, melancholy eyes, foreheads with deep craggy lines, and sagging mouths. They regarded him quizzically, perhaps surprised he'd gotten so far – or maybe they were impressed. Their leaves swished, the wind – a staccato whistle – a quickening heartbeat.

Keene took a deep breath. One last rest, and then they had to get home.

He took off his backpack. Bunch's dry food and biscuits were soggy and ruined, and the chocolate soaked and probably inedible. His sandwich was battered but dry. He unwrapped it, began to lift it to his mouth, then pulled it apart and fed Bunch the ham and cheese and ate the bread himself. He finished with a gulp of juice, and gave Bunch a drink from the bottle of water.

Hurry …

Keene shot to his feet. One of the gum trees had spoken.

Hurry …

This time from behind, then again, and again, until Keene was surrounded. The wind's tempo pounded now, a solitary chorus, deep and insistent, reverberating in his chest and into the pit of his stomach that washed away his exhaustion as it filled him with a newfound strength and urgency.

Hurry hurry hurry hurry hurry hurry hurry hurry hurry hurry hurry hurry …

The faces within the gum trees sharpened; the soil around their roots churned. Their branches jangled and crackled until leaves showered Keene, at first emerald green, but as they drifted through the air they flared to a pale orange, then darkened to a sullen brown as they hit the ground and disintegrated.

Hurryhurryhurryhurryhurryhurryhurryhurryhurry hurryhurryhurryhurryhurryhurryhurryhurryhurry …

Keene slung his backpack over one shoulder. Something banged overhead – a branch had straightened and reached out to its fellow gum trees. Other cracks echoed. Roots ploughed from the earth and branches intertwined to form an archway that lead to the road.

'Thank you …!' Keene said.

The faces in the gum trees bulged as he passed them and their voices implored him individually, some deep, others gravelly, some whispers, some rich, some sharp – a chorus that drove him until he felt the wind under his pumping arms and his feet were moving so fast they barely touched the ground. He laughed at Bunch who loped alongside him, his tongue hanging from his mouth.

'Faster, Bunch! Faster!'

They burst out onto the road and into two balls of brightening light. Tyres screeched as a big brown Ford swung towards them and arced across the road, the rear bumper pivoting centimetres from Keene's face. The car juddered to a halt and the front door opened. Doctor Ward shot out, his bushy eyebrows arching as he rushed up.

'Keene?'

'Hi, Doctor Ward!'

'What're you doing out here? Don't you realise what's going on?'

Doctor Ward closed the distance in several strides, kneeled, and grabbed him by the shoulders. Bunch growled. Doctor Ward's hands loosened, although he didn't release Keene.

'Does your father know you're out here?'

Keene shook his head.

'My God … I was on the way to your house.'

Keene grinned. 'You can take us home!' That would save a lot of time.

Doctor Ward looked at Bunch. He would be just like Dad. Dad never wanted Bunch inside the house when he was wet either. Only Mum changed his mind. Then Keene and Dad would take Bunch into the bathroom and dry him with a towel. There were no bathrooms or towels here, though.

'Please!' Keene said.

'Wait a moment.'

Doctor Ward rummaged around in the back of his car and pulled out two grey blankets. He wrapped one around Keene. Keene pulled it tight, although it scratched at his neck. He looked back to see how it fluttered behind him just like a cape would. Doctor Ward tried to dry Bunch with the other, although Bunch span and made it impossible. Keene giggled. Doctor Ward finally gave up and laid the blanket across the back seat.

'Come on.'

Keene unwrapped his blanket so he could set his backpack on the floor of the passenger seat. Wings flapped above him – the owl, sailing overhead, past an oblivious Doctor Ward, and down the road. Keene waved once, clasped the blanket, and climbed into the car, while Bunch jumped into the back. Doctor Ward closed the doors behind them.

The inside of the car was warm. Hot air blared into Keene's face. More grey blankets lay on the floor in the back, as well as Doctor Ward's leather bag. Soft music filled the car: slow and doleful, the singers lamenting something about the sound of silence.

Doctor Ward slid into the driver's seat and slammed his door shut. His hands closed around the steering wheel and he glanced back at Bunch, then smiled at Keene.

'Ready to go?'

Keene nodded.

Doctor Ward looked back at Bunch. 'Are you ready, Bunch?'

Bunch shook; his fur sprayed water all over the car's interior. Keene laughed. Doctor Ward scowled and shielded himself with his hand until Bunch was done. Satisfied, Bunch lay down on the back seat and lowered his face on his paws. Doctor Ward fetched another of the blankets, scrunched it up, and used it to wipe the windscreen dry.

'I think it's time we were on our way,' he said.

Mum

Keene knew every turn and tree on the drive home. It was the same road he took to and from school every day, but now it didn't seem as long. He could walk it. Dad and Mum would see him off, waving from the veranda. When he got back, Dad would be working in the yard and Mum in the kitchen. Bunch would race from the veranda to greet him.

By the time Doctor Ward steered his big Ford around the final corner, the clouds had finally begun to scatter, and sunlight glimmered off the wet tiles of the roof. The fallen tree lay morosely in the front yard now, the surviving shard blackened but defiant. Without the gum to obscure it, the hole in the top of the house exposed Keene's bedroom for all to see. He wouldn't be able to sleep there tonight. A helicopter buzzed overhead. Keene watched it until it disappeared.

As Doctor Ward pulled the car into the drive, Dad and Yvonne emerged from the house and waited on the veranda. Doctor Ward parked the car and turned the engine off. Keene opened the door and sprang out, Bunch close behind. Dad seemed taller, his chest broad, his shoulders wide; he stormed down the veranda, his nostrils flaring, as frightening as the shadow itself now. He seized Keene by the arms. Bunch fell flat on the ground, ears reared back.

'Where have you been?' Dad's grip tightened. 'Where did you go?'

'I—'

'Where did you find him?'

Doctor Ward approached from the driver's side of the car, Keene's backpack hanging low from one hand. 'Down the road. By the cemetery.'

'Don't you know what's going on out there?' Dad's hands clawed into Keene's shoulders. 'Don't you know what's going on here? *Don't you?*'

'Dad, I—'

'Come on!'

Dad grabbed Keene by the wrist, and jerked him towards the house. Keene shrieked.

'Dad—' he said.

'Nolan—' Yvonne said.

Dad stomped past her, and dragged Keene down the hall and into the downstairs bathroom. He planted Keene in the shower. Keene gasped as cold water hit him, but it wasn't long before it was steaming. Dad stripped him – throwing the clothes into the tub – as mud streamed from Keene and twirled down the drain. Yvonne appeared behind him with a fresh set of clothes and Keene's slippers. Bunch curled in a corner, muck pooling from his coat.

Showers were usually time-consuming, but within minutes Dad had scrubbed him clean and dried him with a coarse towel. Keene cringed as Dad dressed him, thrusting his legs into the cuffs of pants, his arms into a shirt, then a jacket, and finally his feet into his slippers. Keene brushed away an errant tear. Yvonne, in the doorway, grew misty-eyed.

'Come on,' Dad said.

'What about Bunch?'

'We'll worry about Bunch later.'

Yvonne stepped aside as Dad hauled Keene from the bathroom. Doctor Ward waited at the foot of the stairs, Keene's backpack at his feet.

'Wait!' Keene said. He tried to wrench his hand free, but Dad's grip was too tight.

'Your mother's waiting—'

Keene yanked his whole body and fell back through the bathroom doorway. Yvonne kneeled to help him, but he shrugged her off and rifled through his clothes in the tub. He held his breath as he found the first jacket pocket empty, but from the second he pulled the pendant. Dad twisted him around.

'Keene, how dare …?' Dad's gaze fell on the pendant swinging from Keene's hand. His mouth dropped open. The pendant sparkled between them.

Keene burst past him, sidestepped Yvonne, and trod on Doctor Ward's foot as he flew up the stairs. He heard Bunch bark once, then Bunch's paws clip across the floorboards and the steps.

Averil waited in Mum's doorway, hands behind her back. 'Hello, Keene,' she said, voice low.

'Hi, Averil.'

Keene closed his hand around the pendant and entered Mum's bedroom. Although the room was unusually bright, sunlight dappling the walls and highlighting the colour in some of his pictures which hung there, shadows flickered from the corners of the room and grasped for Mum's bed.

Mum's face was pasty, her eyes dark. 'Keene …'

Keene went straight to the stereo. Mozart's Piano Concerto 21 was still in the player. He switched it on.

The number '2' lit up on the LCD screen. He pushed PLAY. The second movement of the concerto filled the room, and now even the shadows flickered and reared back.

'Mum,' Keene said, as he climbed up onto the edge of the bed. Bunch lay down just outside the doorway as Dad approached. Yvonne and Doctor Ward remained discreetly behind him. Averil joined them. Yvonne kneeled and stroked Bunch, who'd begun to whine.

'What did you do today?' Mum asked.

He had to strain to hear her. She lifted her hand, but it barely came up from her chest. Keene kissed her on the head.

'I went and got you a surprise.'

'A surprise?' A smile tugged at her mouth. 'Your picture?'

'Better!'

Keene opened his hand. The pendant fell out, jagged upon the cord around his palm, bounced, then swung back and forth. Mum gaped and her lips pursed, but there was no sound.

'Kee, how did you ...?'

'I went and got it. Me and Bunch.'

Keene laid the pendant on her chest. Her hand closed on his. She was cold. Her chest heaved, her breath a rasp.

'That was very sweet of you, Kee.'

'Now you can be better.'

'Better?'

'The pendant will make you better.'

'No, Kee …'

'But you only got sick because you lost it.'

'No …'

'Get better now, Mum.' Keene shook her by the shoulder.

'Kee, I'm not going to get better.'

'What do you mean?'

'I have to go …'

Keene's hand trembled above the pendant. He lay by Mum's side, rested his head against her temple and put one arm across her chest. He could feel it rise. She had to stay. Her hand opened and closed on the pendant as it lay on her chest.

'Mum …'

'Kee …' Her eyelashes flickered upon his. 'You'll be good. You'll be strong.'

'What, Mum? I don't know what you mean.'

'Kee …? I've been very sick—'

'You'll be all right now.'

'I've been very sick, and I have to go. I have to leave you now.'

'Mum …?'

'But even though I have to go … I'll always be with you. Always, Kee. Always. Do you understand? *Always.*'

'Mum?'

'Love you. Always …'

'Please?' Keene pressed the pendant into her chest. It would glow now and destroy the shadows, although understanding of what she was telling him began to sink in. 'Get better?' His voice was a whisper. '*Please* get better …?' He shook her by the shoulder once more. 'Mum?'

Mum didn't respond. A tear streamed down her cheek. The brightness in her eyes faded until they became flat and dull. Keene pushed himself up. Somebody sobbed behind him. Bunch howled.

'Mum?'

She neither moved nor answered. Her hand had formed a loose cave around the pendant, dull and orange on her still chest – her chest had never been still. She'd never been still. Even at her sickest, she'd always been here with him.

'Mum?' Keene shook her again.

A large, strong hand closed on the back of his head. 'Kee …'

'No.' Keene said. '*No!*'

He grabbed the pendant and hurled it. Dad reached for him. Keene jumped from the bed. The pendant lay in the middle of the hardwood floor; it reminded him of his toys when his room became a mess – not only discarded and forgotten but unimportant.

'Kee!' Dad said.

'No!'

Keene stomped the pendant, his slipper flapping, mocking applause that angered him until Dad caught him and lifted him. Keene punched and kicked and screamed, but Dad's grip was strong.

'Keene, Keene, Keene,' Dad said.

Strength seeped from Keene's limbs. He buried his face in Dad's shoulder. Dad bounced him, and ran a hand up and down his back. Keene blinked through tears. Mum lay on the bed as if she was taking a nap and might wake at any moment. Sometimes, she used to pretend sleep and then jolt awake to scare him. Keene closed his eyes. That would happen. That's what she was doing. When he opened his eyes, she would make a scary face and boo him and tickle him, just like she used to before she became sick.

When he opened his eyes, everything would be fine.

When he opened his eyes, she would be okay.

Keene clenched his eyes tighter.

Home

Dad's bedroom was the biggest and brightest bedroom in the house, with a window in the front and another in the side. There'd always been a warmth about the pastel blue walls, but now they were like faces of ice caught in a perpetual expression of disbelief and shock.

Keene blinked through tears as Dad laid him on the bed. Bunch jumped up and curled at his feet, his muddy coat staining the covers. Dad regarded him with only the mildest curiosity, then lay down and put a large hand on Keene's chest. Keene could feel his fluttering heartbeat bounce off Dad's callused palm.

'It'll be okay,' he said.

Keene closed his eyes.

When he opened them again, it was night. He'd slept, although he didn't know how long. It mustn't have been too late, or Dad would've been here too. Bunch, still curled at his feet, lifted his head. The wind whipped at the windows so they groaned in their panes.

He got out of bed and drifted onto the landing, Bunch following. The door to Mum's bedroom was closed. Keene swung it open, the door's squeal a solitary lament. The room was hazy shapes that had once been so familiar, but now seemed unreal. The corner was empty – there was no sense of anything being there. Mum's bed had been stripped clean. The rest of the room was bare – no signs of Mum's clothes, or her medicine, or her CDs. Even Keene's pictures were gone. He eased the door closed and crept down the stairs.

Light seeped from the kitchen and lapped onto the hall floorboards. Dad sat at the kitchen table, beer in one hand, the index finger of his other hand tracing a shape on the table top. A greeting died on Keene's lips as he got closer – the shape Dad was tracing was the pendant, laid out flat, the cord a big messy loop, the citrine dull.

Keene wondered why Dad would even bother with the pendant. It had no power. It hadn't fixed Mum, and if it hadn't fixed Mum its absence certainly hadn't been the reason she'd gotten sick. Keene understood what Dad and Yvonne had tried to tell him: some things just *were*. Like night falling. Like the sun coming up. Like Mum getting sick.

Now the pendant was just a gift he'd given Mum. He remembered how happy she'd been when he'd brought it home. He tried to hold onto that – that he'd made her happy. Maybe that was what Dad was thinking, too – about when Mum had been happy.

His eyes glistened as he drank from his beer. Empties lined the sink. The radio was off. Everybody else must've gone home. He clutched the pendant – clutched it as tight as Keene had. Keene wanted to run to him, throw his arms around him. He took a single step forward, but when the floorboard creaked, he dashed back into the darkness. Dad looked up. Bunch remained in the hall, head down, tail wagging.

'Go to bed, Bunch,' Dad said.

Keene fled back upstairs and into bed. He pulled up the covers as Bunch trotted in, jumped up to join him, circled on the spot, and lay down, his sigh plaintive.

'I know, Bunch.'

Keene was sure he wouldn't sleep, or that if he did it would be filled with nightmares, but he knew nothing until the chopping of wood woke him in the morning. Bunch, fur matted and mud caked all over his body, greeted him with a wagging tail.

Hopping from bed, Keene crept up to the window. The workers were back, chopping the fallen tree, loading branches into their truck, and stacking a woodpile by the side of the house. Other workers approached the shard of the gum with shovels. In the drive was Yvonne's truck; behind it was Mr. Obling's black car. Mr. Obling and Dad stood in front of it, talking.

Keene left the bedroom and stopped at Mum's bedroom door. He reached for the doorknob – no, he'd checked it last night. She wasn't there. But he still twisted the doorknob. The door swung open noiselessly. The bedroom was empty. The sunlight that filled it was unnatural – a golden blur of mist that seemed to pulse sheepishly at being discovered.

He went downstairs and, with Bunch in tow, into the kitchen. Yvonne was there. She smiled at him.

'How're you, Keene?'

Keene shrugged.

'Some cereal?'

Keene sat at the kitchen table and shrugged again. Bunch sat on the floor.

Yvonne fixed him some cereal and put it in front of him.

'Thank you,' he said.

'I think we have a job to do today.'

'What?'

'I think we really need to wash Bunch. What do you say?'

Keene shrugged. 'Okay.'

When the time came, Bunch hid under the dining room coffee table, and Keene had to coax him out. Bunch whined all the way to the bathroom, digging his paws into the floor, but once they wrestled him into the tub, he resigned himself to a thorough scrubbing, although it took several buckets of hot water to rinse his coat. When they were done, they used three towels to dry him. Bunch shook himself and sprayed them. Keene wiped his face dry with the cuff of his sleeve.

'Maybe you should give him a treat for being such a good dog while we washed him,' Yvonne said. 'I'm going to clean out your bag, okay?'

'Okay.'

Keene fetched a biscuit from the kitchen and fed it to Bunch. Yvonne joined them shortly, Keene's backpack in one hand, and his opened lunchbox in the other. Inside the lunchbox, the sagging orchid lay in a bed of wet soil.

'What's this, Keene?'

'I was going to give it to …' Keene sniffled.

Yvonne understood, and the smile she offered was assuring – she wasn't so bad, the way she was always trying to help.

'How about we plant it in the garden?' she said.

'Will it be okay?'

'I don't know. But we can try our best to help it, can't we?'

They went out to the front yard. Keene expected the spiders would still be there, but they were nowhere to be seen. He picked up the trowel and dug a hole for the orchid. Yvonne handed it to him and he slotted it in. Together, they packed the hole with dirt. The flower's blue petals were striking against the wild backdrop of red roses, but its stem slumped.

'I don't want it to die,' Keene said.

Yvonne's lips drew thin.

Keene bolted into the house and retreated to the dining room, running his dirty fingers over the keys of the piano. Mozart's concertos ran through his mind, alongside memories of sitting with Mum on the piano stool and playing together. He closed the piano lid.

His drawing and pencils littered the coffee table. He was meant to show his picture to Mum but had forgotten. He grabbed the paper, scrunched it up and threw it across the room. Bunch pranced after it, nudged it with his nose, then panted at Keene.

Keene remained sullen over a lunch of sandwiches with Yvonne and Dad, and quiet throughout the rest of the day. During the evening, he and Dad watched television until he drifted off and Dad carried him to bed. When he awoke, he charged from the house still in his pyjamas and checked the orchid, but it was still wilting.

He started to move away, then stopped. The roses weren't right – not this way, tangled, untamed, and like they'd been caught in the middle of a scream. He yanked the clippers from the soil, closed his eyes, and pictured the roses neat and square – just the way Mum had taught him. Then he began to trim, diffidently at first, but then with greater surety.

It became his routine for the next three days: he would rush down and check on the orchid. Then he would take the clippers and continue to trim the roses. Sometimes, he had to get up on the veranda and reach through the spindles to cut the tops of the roses. And one time, he brought out a kitchen chair and stood on it. Slowly, the roses took shape, until he was sure Mum would be proud of them. They weren't as pretty as when she cut them, but it was the best he could do, and he felt they were happy now that they had some order.

On the fourth day, Dad laid out Keene's black pants, a shirt, and a black jacket. Keene glared at the clothes, then fled into his shattered bedroom. It had been cleaned now – the floor had been swept, the bed stripped, and a huge sheet of plastic put up to cover the hole in the wall where the window had once been. Keene sat on his bed with his knees drawn to his chest. The wind splattered against the plastic. Dad knocked, startling Keene. But of course Dad would come. It was just Dad and him now. And Bunch.

'Kee?'

Keene didn't answer.

'Come out, please.'

'No.'

'Kee, now please. It's okay.'

'*No.*'

'Keene! Now!'

The door swung open and Dad came in, clothes in hand. Keene ran for the closet. Dad caught him by the wrist and wordlessly dressed him. Keene protested and cried throughout, but Dad was implacable.

They got into the van, Bunch jumping into the backseat. When Dad started the engine, music blared – the sort of rock and roll with lots of guitar that Dad always listened to. Dad switched the radio off. CDs were crammed in the change compartment. Dad pulled one out at random and fed it into the CD player. As he reversed from the drive, slow piano filled the van.

'This music's stupid,' Keene said.

'It's not stupid.'

'You don't like it.'

'Who said that?'

Keene scowled. 'You never listened to it.'

'I like lots of different things.'

'You don't like this.'

'I love Mozart,' Dad said with a light-heartedness he'd never used when talking about this music.

'This is Beethoven.' It was – the 'Emperor' concerto, second movement.

'I might not know this music like you and Mum, but I do like it.'

Keene folded his arms across his chest.

'I think you should try to keep liking it, too.'

'Why?'

'Because it's something you can always have with Mum.'

'Mum's gone!'

'But she gave you this. It's a part of her she wanted you to keep.'

Keene looked away. Passing trees were bleary.

'You should keep playing, too.'

Keene wiped his nose.

'If you want to.'

They drove to the church in town and parked out back. Keene didn't want to leave the van so Dad plucked him out, set him down, and then kneeled by him, straightening out his shirt. Keene glowered at him, although he knew it wasn't nice. Dad smiled a tiny smile – Keene thought he might've imagined it – brushed the side of Keene's head, then rose to his full height. He rolled down the window all the way so Bunch could have some fresh air while he waited.

Hand in hand, Keene and Dad walked around to the front of the church. Neither looked up, nor spoke, even when they greeted Averil, and then Yvonne. Standing behind Yvonne was Ashley, her red hair braided and tied with a ribbon every bit as blue as the orchid. All three of them were dressed in black.

'Hi, Keene,' Ashley said.

'Hi, Ashley.'

'I'm sorry about your mum, Keene,' Ashley said.

She hugged him. Keene went rigid, although she was soft and warm against him. It was nice, but a stupid nice he wasn't used to. When Ashley let go, he grimaced, although he also wished she wouldn't go too far.

Dad marched them to the front pew. Mum's coffin rested by the podium, a picture of Mum on top. The top half of the coffin was open, although from here Keene couldn't see her. He didn't know if he wanted to, but had no choice when Dad lifted him and carried him to the coffin's side after the priest's service.

Mum had make-up on now – like she used to – although somebody else must've painted it on her to try make her look the way she had when she was alive. She wore a violet dress and the pendant hung around her neck and rested on her chest. Dad kissed her on the lips. When he rose, tears streamed down his face. Keene had never seen him cry.

'Keene?'

Keene tilted in Dad's arms and pecked Mum on the cheek. She was icy and, although she wore perfume there was a bitter undercurrent that had never been there before – like the stuff Mum used when she mopped the floors. The expression on her face was missing anything Keene had ever known about her.

'It's not her,' he said softly.

Dad carried Keene back to the van and put him in the passenger seat, before getting into the driver's seat. He started the engine, then switched it off. Keene was about to prompt him when Dad started the engine once more.

They drove to the cemetery, turning from the main road and onto a narrow dirt road. When they parked in the small lot, Keene left the van voluntarily, although it was curiosity that drove him. While the grass was wet, the rest of the cemetery was intact. All the headstones were in place and there were no signs of the damage the shadow had done. Even the sky – now so plain and blue, but for the blaring sun – showed no memory of the storm yesterday.

Mum's grave rested on the hill under the crooked willow, although the plot wasn't the same one he'd seen. The others joined them and they stood reverently – Bunch lying with his chin nestled on his paws – as the priest delivered his benediction. Keene trembled through the service, his teeth chattering. He didn't want to listen, but couldn't stop himself from watching the coffin being lowered. Dad knelt and threw some dirt into the grave.

'Keene?'

Keene shook his head.

'Please?'

'No.'

Yvonne held out something – a folded paper that was all crumpled. 'Maybe you want to give her this.'

Keene took the paper and only had to partly open it to recognise it was his drawing. 'Why?' He started to scrunch it, then stopped. 'She won't see it.'

'She's always with you, Keene, and she'll like that she has it.'

'It's a good idea, Kee,' Dad said.

Keene dropped the paper. It fluttered and looped into the grave, landing on top of the coffin. Dad rested a hand on his back. Yvonne offered one of her half-smiles. Averil knelt and gave him a hug and Ashley kissed him on the cheek. Keene wiped it off with the back of his hand.

Dad guided him back to the van and they climbed in. 'Ready to go home?'

'I guess.'

They did not speak, the second movement of Beethoven's 'Emperor' concerto their only company. When they rounded the corner, Keene focused on the hole in the house. How long before he had his bedroom back? He couldn't sleep with Dad forever. Dad parked the van in the drive and switched off the engine. The van was too quiet now.

'What're we going to do?' Keene asked.

Dad smiled. 'We'll work something out, Kee.' He planted a hand on Keene's shoulder. 'We'll be okay. Come on.'

Keene got out of the van. The roses in the flowerbed stood to attention, like they were beaming with pride. As he got closer, he saw it: the orchid was tall and straight today, the leaves a deep azure blue, with splashes of violet through their centre. He reached out to stroke it, but pulled back. No. It just needed to grow.

'Keene?' Dad said. He unlocked the front door and went into the house. Bunch waited, tail swishing.

'Coming!' Keene said.

He followed Dad into the house.

Acknowledgements

This story took forever to write. It was one that came with great difficulty, often only progressing ten or twenty words at a time, with other passages (including a big part of the start) needing to be rewritten. I pushed on, my only companion Mozart's Piano Concerto 21 – the first movement epitomised Keene's spirit

Once I had the story down, a lot of people contributed to the construction of this universe: a big thank you to Ryan O'Neill, Kim Lock, Tom O'Connell, and Blaise van Hecke, who all read an early draft of this story, when it was initially known as 'Shadow and Hope.'

In learning about the Nolans, I also wrote two short stories.

The first was a prequel story, 'Pendant', which deals with Deidre's diagnosis, and also explores some of the events mentioned here, such as the fire in the bush, and the visit to Miller's Pond. A big thanks to Blaise van Hecke (again), Kim Lock (again), Bel Woods, and Laurie Steed, who challenged me to learn more about this world. Thanks also to editor Effie Sapuridis, who accepted 'Pendant' for publication in the young adult literary journal *fterotalogia* and worked with me through revision.

The other short story, 'The Owl at the Window', ran concurrent to this story, but told it from Deidre's point of view. Some of the events are the same, such as her final conversation with Keene. But we get to see what she feels and thinks, and how Keene retrieving the pendant actually is a gift for her – just not the gift Keene thought it was going to be. Thanks (again) to Blaise, Kim, Laurie, and Ryan.

This novella was originally written in 2013, and the short stories in 2013 and 2014, so they've germinated with me a long, long time. They've each been repeatedly revised in the intervening years. But it always helps when you have good, talented people around you who sync to your wavelength and see what you're trying to do, then challenge you constructively, but also teach you something. Keene's world would be lesser without them.

In bringing the novella to publication, thank you to Anais Thornbury, Sam Stevens, Alyse Clarke, Tara Cairnduff, Laura McCluskey, and Blaise van Hecke – the latter two also for their considered structural editing. All of them showed me a different facet of the story that I needed to explore further. Hopefully, that shows.

A big thank you to Kev Howlett, for the cover image, and Blaise van Hecke for putting the cover together. And a special thank you to Blaise, who reads all my stuff (as it shows) and always provides thoughtful feedback.

While this is the end of *this* book, it's not the end of the story. I plan to revisit Keene's life at periodic intervals, so watch out for the next novella.

About the Author

Lazaros Zigomanis has wanted to tell stories since he read JRR Tolkien's *The Hobbit*, and then *The Lord of the Rings* when he was 11-12 years of age. Ever since, he's always been writing something and trying to tell *some* story.

He's had stories and articles published extensively in various print and digital journals, as well as three screenplays optioned.

His first novel – the adult version known as *Pride*, and the Young Adult version known as *Song of the Curlew* – is a story about chasing dreams, how the choices we make shape our lives, family and community, first love, and racism, all set to the backdrop of a country football league over the course of one extraordinary football season.

He is currently working on a new novel where mental health is the key theme.

Luke Miggs wants more than small-town life: the grind of chores on the family farm, playing footy, and drinks with friends. Like maybe doing something about his crush on Amanda Hunt, a barmaid at the local pub who's smart, funny, and ambitious. Or playing footy in the big league. At eighteen, it can't be too late, can it?

When Adam Pride emerges from the night and tells the Curlews he wants to play for them, everything begins to change. But with that change comes a mystery – who is Adam, and what is his link to Claude Rankin, the tyrannical captain-coach of the reigning champions?

Song of the Curlew is a story of friendship, bonds, and coming of age, and how the choices of our past can come back to shape our future.

'A must-read for all who love a good ol' game of footy and believe in the unbelievable.'
Kathrine 'Kat' Clarke
Writer, Artist, Cultural Advisor

Take a journey into the minds of thirteen of Australia's most promising new and emerging writers as they delve into stories that explore the bonds of friendship and family, love and heartbreak, and coming of age and the loss of innocence.

Featuring A.S. Patric (winner of the 2016 Miles Franklin for *Black Rock, White City*), Ryan O'Neill (winner of the 2017 Australian Prime Minister's Literary Award for *Their Brilliant Careers*), Emilie Collyer (acclaimed playwright), and many more, *13 Stories* is a bold, fearless anthology that's sure to offer something for every reader.

Lose yourself in the world of the short story, and revel in the craft of these talented authors – names you're sure to see more of in the future.

The road to Tralfamadore is bathed in river water

Blaise van Hecke
Stories from a gypsy childhood

In the early 1970s, a single mother and her four children find themselves alone on the east coast of New South Wales. They join the 'Back to the Earth Movement' at the idyllic land known as 'Tralfamadore'.

For Blaise and her siblings, as well as children from the other homes scattered in the bush amongst nine dwellings, life is unrestrained and full of adventure.

The Road to Tralfamadore is Bathed in River Water is a memoir that depicts a childhood full of both naïvety and wisdom during an era of radical social change.

'A beautifully rendered portrait of a place and time, a family and a community. Nostalgic, tender – and yet clear-eyed.'
Inga Simpson
Understory: a life with trees

Questions for Discussion

1. The book's dedication reads: 'To never giving up hope'. Can you identify any times when Keene may have felt hopeless, and how he overcame it?
2. Keene's mother is very ill for the duration of the book. In what ways can illness affect those other than the person who is ill?
3. What is 'imagery'? Can you outline three examples of imagery in the book?
4. The appearance of the crone initially scares Keene, before he learns that she is trying to help him. What can this tell us about forming judgements based on appearance?
5. A 'hero's journey' is a very common story structure. In which ways do you think *The Shadow in the Wind* exemplifies this structure?
6. The book describes storms in great detail. Why do you think the author has included storms in this novel?
7. How does music serve to enhance Keene's relationship with his mother?
8. Why does Keene see the amber pendant as symbolic of his mother's illness?
9. Keene describes shadows as overtaking his mother's room. Why do you think the author is including this imagery?
10. Keene's mother says that she will always be with him. In what ways can people still be with us after death?
11. Why do you think Keene rebels against Yvonne, and what leads to his perception of her to change?
12. Keene leaves his house to search for the pendant, despite his father's express instruction to stay at home. Do you think that prohibited (or illegal) acts can ever be justified?
13. What are some examples of Keene's father making compromises to make Keene happy?

14. What is 'nostalgia'? Can you think of any examples of nostalgia in *The Shadow in the Wind?*
15. Who was your favourite character, and why?
16. Stories are often divided into 'good' and 'bad' characters. Do you think that there is a 'bad' character in this novel? What elements of 'bad' are present in the main characters?
17. Sometimes when people very close to us are sick, we can enter into denial of how bad things are. Do you think there are any examples of denial in this novel?
18. The gum trees are described as having 'faces'. Can you find any other examples of personification?
19. What do you think IT is?
20. What is 'metaphor'? In what way is Keene learning to swim a metaphor for something else?
21. The novel is set in the Australian bush. What elements of the text tell us this?
22. Can you identify a 'turning point' in the novel, when things begin to change?
23. Do you think Keene and his father's relationship will improve, or worsen? Why?
24. What do you think is the most frightening part of the story?
25. Something that is 'supernatural' is something that is beyond the laws of science or nature. What supernatural elements can you identify in this novel?
26. Keene asks his dad to read *Hansel and Gretel*. In what ways is that story similar to this one?
27. Keene draws his backyard sunny, with a perfect blue sky and a neat rose garden. Do you ever use art to express yourself? In what ways?
28. Why is Keene nervous to prune the roses by himself? Have you ever been nervous to undertake a new or confusing task? If so, how did you overcome it?
29. Keene's Dad uses music to 'fill the silence'. Why do you think he might want to avoid silence?
30. What do you think is the importance of the comparison between darkness and light in the novel?

Pinion Press is an imprint of Busybird Publising.

We specialise in publishing a handful of our own titles yearly, trying to combine quality and enjoyability with some altruistic outcome, e.g. raising awareness for a particular condition (as our glorious coffee table photography book, *Walk With Me* – a journal of Kev Howlett's trek up to Mount Everest Base Camp and back – raised awareness of Charcot-Marie-Tooth disease), and/or donate a portion of proceeds for books to various foundations, such as Women Helping Other Women, Breast Cancer Victoria, the Prostate Cancer Foundation, the Epilepsy Foundation, Vision Australia, and the Indigenous Literacy Foundation.

Busybird Publishing is a boutique micropublisher based in the heart of Montmorency, Victoria.

We help authors self-publish. A fee-for-service self-publisher, we make no claims on rights or royalties, and are determined to make sure our authors have a pleasurable, gratifying, and educational journey.

We also run workshops on various forms of writing (fiction, nonfiction, memoir), publishing, and photography, organise writing retreats; host a monthly Open Mic Night (the third Wednesday of every month); and hold competitions to help aspiring writers get published or win mentoring.

To learn more about Busybird Publishing, check out our website at **www.busybird.com.au**.